Helen Dickens

Wild Wood

A novel. Vol. 1

Helen Dickens

Wild Wood
A novel. Vol. 1

ISBN/EAN: 9783337067168

Printed in Europe, USA, Canada, Australia, Japan

Cover: Foto ©Andreas Hilbeck / pixelio.de

More available books at **www.hansebooks.com**

WILD WOOD.

A NOVEL.

IN THREE VOLUMES.

BY

HELEN DICKENS.

"Into the blithe and breathing air,
Into the solemn wood,
Solemn and silent everywhere
Nature with folded hands seemed there,
Kneeling at her evening prayer,
Like one in prayer I stood."

VOL. I.

LONDON :

T. CAUTLEY NEWBY, PUBLISHER,

30, WELBECK STREET, CAVENDISH SQUARE.

1872.

POPULAR NEW NOVEL.

In Three Vols.   Price 31s. 6d.

SECOND EDITION.

FIRM IN THE STRUGGLE.

By EMMA PICKERING,

Author of "Forsaking all Others," &c.

"Miss Pickering always writes like a lady of education and refinement. The dialogue of 'Firm in the Struggle' is clever, abounding in smartness and piquancy. Amongst trees, and flowers, and quiet country scenes, she is thoroughly at home, and these she sketches with happy effect and truthfulness."—ALBION.

"The contemptuous scorn of the usually gentle Avice, the thorough goodness of Hugh, or the affectation of Maud are drawn most naturally, while Lily and Bessie are perfect characters."—JOHN BULL.

"The story is extremely interesting, and never flags for a single page. We scarcely know a fiction of modern times in which the characters are so well sketched and sustained. Many of the descriptions of country life and scenery are quite equal to those so admirably depicted in 'Adam Bede.'"—DAILY GUARDIAN.

"Miss Pickering's truthful pictures of country life and scenery are not surpassed by any of the female novelists of the present time."—BRIGHTON EXAMINER.

"This novel is fair and fresh as May flowers, and deserves for its ability of treatment and purity of tone the highest praise. All the characters are well and evenly drawn, and show a great harmony of treatment. It is a story of life: full of life's sorrows, temptations, joys, and triumphs."—DRAWING-ROOM GAZETTE.

"The skill of the authoress has allowed her to rise into the higher regions of imaginative lore."—BELL'S MESSENGER.

"Interesting, well written and wholesome. It contains a number of natural incidents clearly described. Humour and pathos show that Miss Pickering possesses the power to enlist the sympathies and command the attention of her readers, while the regular succession of events, and the unbroken thread of the narrative, never allow the interest to flag."—THE BOOKSELLER.

"'Firm in the Struggle' is entirely free from the worst blemishes of modern fictions.'—OBSERVER.

—Railways, postages—in a word, all the numerous facilities of the age—have almost annihilated distance, and, as a natural result, caused an individual trade between country customers and London establishments. Those who do not visit town, so as to select and purchase directly, send for patterns from which they can give their orders. But as all apparent advantages on the one hand have more or less their corresponding drawbacks, so this system is not without its bane. Pushing tradesmen make a market by offering goods at lower rates than they can possibly be sold at to realise a fair profit. The bait traps the unreflective, and the result is that the receipts *en masse* are not equal to the tempting samples. There is no new invention in this; it has been practised in wholesale merchandise and by candidates for contracts, as the proverb hath it, since there were hills and valleys. But we grieve to add it is sometimes resorted to by those whom one would credit for more integrity. Ladies, therefore, need exercise caution, and place confidence only in houses of old-established fame, for rapidly-made businesses are not generally reliable. And to what does this assertion amount more than to the fact that nothing great can be effected not only without labour but without time, and that Rome was not built, as the old saying says, in a day? Messrs. Jay, of Regent-street, whose name is well known amongst the few on the l.st of *bond fide* establishments in the metropolis, have adopted a plan for assisting country ladies in choosing for themselves London fashions and fabrics. And their customers may rest assured that they will thus be enabled to obtain goods of every quality, both low and high priced, at the most reasonable terms—that is, the terms of small profits for quick returns—and that they may firmly rely upon the thoroughly corresponding character of samples and supplies.—From the *Court Journal.*

WILD WOOD.

CHAPTER I.

THE sun was setting one Tuesday afternoon in September—Wild Wood clock had struck four, and the firing had not yet ceased. The keepers and others had been blazing away all day, and there were many orphans and widows amongst the birds that strutted in the woods. No place looks prettier than when the sun is on it;—and had anyone been gazing at Wild Wood on this particular Tuesday afternoon, they would have been specially pleased by the sight. It was wrapped in a mantle of gold,—it was a noble old house, with its courtyard and moss-grown ivy-covered turret; the windows were deeply set in the solid red stone, and most of the rooms possessed those delicious inventions—window seats, nicely cushioned and roomy. Sight-seers were invariably struck with the imposing appearance of Wild Wood. It looked grand standing in all its proud glory on the top of a green hill, where strawberries grew in abundance. At a distance it seemed as though the glorious trees in the surrounding woods met over it; but when you had mounted up, they receded, and you saw splendid gardens to the left, and to the right a magnificent grove of yew trees, while all round the woods met the eye. It was a good pull up from the grand entrance, and seats were put for the convenience of short-winded individuals. The walnut and copper beech trees stood in all their majesty on each side of the avenues, and afforded homes for numerous squirrels and birds; and on those hot days—that only the South can boast of—many were the forms stretched beneath their ample shade. The village butcher and baker boys seemed to make to them as a haven of rest. Could these noble kings of the forest have spoken, they would have related the doings of Maldon for generations, and told of the proud old Drevers who never yet cut one of their brethren down to replenish their coffers. Wild Wood was nearly as old as the trees, and reared its eccentric old chimneys, gables, and turrets in scornful contempt on the more modern erections that considered themselves ancient.

As the old Drevers died off, and the new ones took possession and brought the young madams home, sundry little improvements and alterations had been executed in the interior, but the exterior was left to state its age to admiring spectators, like the trees. Had any authority on the subject been asked his opinion, he would have recommended a prop here and a prop there, for several portions of the courtyard and out-buildings looked quite ready to depart from their neighbours. But it was an understood thing that Wild Wood was never to be touched, excepting when it gave way, and then it was to be put together again in the old style.

There was a legend told of a certain Squire Drever, who, to please his wife, consented to pull down an old turret at the east end ; but the owls and ravens which infested the place never ceased screaming, and his lady was found dead in her bed. This brought the Lord of the Manor to his senses, and he had it rebuilt; but the moss or ivy would never make friends with that east turret, and it remained bare ever after in strange contrast to the rest. It was known as the fated turret. The courtyard clock had chimed four, then the clocks in the village, so that for many and many a mile the people knew the hour. A few moments after a graceful figure swept down the oaken staircase in a most becoming costume, and out at the side door to go to the gardens, humming the last new song. This radiant beauty was Miss Lois Drever, the noted county belle.

The Drevers were a good-looking family : but there were two classes. Some took after Madam Drever's family—the Bentons, and, without doubt, they were the most dazzling, and considered by many the most beautiful, especially the female portion. The Drevers were a dark brown, with handsome eyes and extremely intelligent faces ; but they lacked what the Bentons possessed—a delicacy of feature. In the men it amounted to almost effeminacy ; their finely cut features, lovely blue eyes, and yellow locks, almost rendered them " pretty men." But here the strong character and sterling qualities which predominated in the Drever family shone forth, and imparted a more decided tone to their supple dispositions and pretty faces. The Drevers were known as men of great power and ability, coupled with untarnished honour. The women (those who took after the father's side) were cut after the same pattern, only on a much more delicate scale. They had great courage and true womanly hearts, but the common sense seemed to be pretty equally divided,

The present Squire John Reginald Drever was a hale old man in years, but in good health. His wife, Jeanie, was the daughter of Lord Benton, and they had married for love. Their years had been to them but as days, so peacefully had they passed, and now in the decline of life they looked on their children with pleasure and pride.

Theirs was a true English family—large. As the French say, "Ah! but you must come to England to see that." Yes, England is the place to see large families. The Drevers were eight—four boys and four girls;—they were a happy united family; they clung together in twos and twos like most large families. There is something very pleasant in a large family in the country: they are never dull, and all have friends of their own, whom they invite to stay from time to time. Then they have charming skating parties by the light of the moon, or bonfires, and, if Jack Frost does not treat them to his presence, they have dances. If it be summer, there are picnics and nutting parties, without mentioning that detestable and ridiculous game croquet, which people are so fond of. To see that game in its true colours, and properly played, the sides must not be without two or three—" mutton-dressed-lamb-fashion " ladies and a corresponding number of " lean curates." Then to see the ogling, advancing, and retiring performance that goes on is something past all conception. It puts one in mind of Mr. Dousie with a fiddle-stick ready to scrape a " little toon," and his mouth

full of " Now, young ladies, hold your dresses,
and advance, and retire—so." Whereupon Mr.
Dousie slides across the floor on his toes with the
fiddle-stick posed gracefully in the air, and his
face adorned with the everlasting black moustache, turned over the left shoulder, while he leers
insinuatingly at some Miss Somebody. The ladies
who delight in croquet evidently have not forgotten their dancing lessons by the way they
parabasque over the lawn in child's sized boots.
I fancy I hear a whisper—" Be charitable."

About half-past four there is a commotion in
the courtyard consequent upon the return of the
shooting party. It is composed of gentlemen,
keepers, and dogs, but only one Drever—the
oldest son and heir, Durill. The Squire is now
too old to shoot all day, so he came home some
hours before them.

" Well, if you fellows won't come in and have
something, I suppose I shall see you to-morrow ?"

" No, thanks, Drever, it is getting on for five ; but I think there will be a pretty good muster to-morrow, after such capital sport to-day."

" So much the better. Glad to see you all, you know."

Then there was a great deal of laughing, joking, and saying " good-byes," before they trooped off through the Druids Grove, which was the nearest way for most of them. Then Durill Drever turned round, and made for the side entrance ; but before he had reached it, he encountered pretty Lois returning from the gardens. She held a few choice flowers in her hand, and her lovely face with its crown of yellow hair made her look bewitching. There was a great contrast between brother and sister—the one so dark, stern, and handsome ; the other so golden and fairy-like. But Lois was a Benton Drever, like three of the others.

Durill Drever was a mighty man, Lois's yellow

head did not nearly reach his great shoulder as she stood beside him.

"Have they all gone, Durill?"

"Yes; they would not come in. I think some of them asked after you, Lois."

"Did they? much obliged. Were the Hardwicks out, Durill?"

"No; Captain Hardwick is expecting his young brother George down, and I think he went to meet him."

Durill stretched himself.

"They have not got back yet, I suppose, Lois?"

"They! if you mean by 'they'—Judy and the new importations—no; and if I had my way they would stay away. I cannot see why we must be saddled with other people's children. Gilbert got married entirely on his own account to some vulgar girl: he never asked any of our opinions about it, and now he has the cheek to send us two children."

Pretty Lois looked very wrath, and the big man at her side took it coolly.

"Well, we must be kind to the poor little beggars, Lois. They are not to blame for their father being a fool. I wonder what they are like, though?" and he stroked his splendid moustache meditatively.

Like most bachelors of thirty-three, he had a vague idea of children.

"The same as most other children—Minnie's, for instance—cross-tempered," answered the still angry Lois.

"Come, Lois, you are too severe; Minnie's children are not bad-tempered naturally, and when they are it is their mother's fault. She is like you—not suited to them. That Arnold is a bonny little chap."

"Well, I am not so fond of children, I confess, and I don't suppose you will be after we have had these two here a month. They will be an intolerable nuisance."

" Indeed! they are here now, so we shall soon find out. Hush! I think I hear wheels."

" Do you? then good bye. I am off, for they are certain to scream, if at nothing else but your great face."

Off ran Lois, leaving Durill, showing white teeth from ear to ear, to follow more slowly. At the bottom of the stairs Lois ran into a good sensible looking girl, a shade taller than herself, and very like the great fellow she had left in the garden.

" Don't stop me, May. Durill says he hears the carriage, and those infants are sure to make a disturbance. I wish you joy at your end with those children. It is well you have only Durill with you, and Julius is away. If Crispin had been at home, and in the west end, he would have served you out."

" I thought you did not want to be stopped, Lois, and here you are saying what you have no need to say. The children must go somewhere, they cannot sleep upon the roof, and it was Judy that fixed upon those two rooms more than I."

"Judy? yes, indeed, she would like to turn us all upside down because they are her dear Gilbert's children."

"Well! I don't think you need make such a fuss, Lois; you will not miss your sleep, or be distressed in any way."

"There, May, you are vexed I can see."

"I am not over pleased, I must confess," replied May, raising her full brown eyes to the worrying Lois, who seemed quite happy mounted up three stairs, and laughing at May's sober face. "I think you are getting very selfish, Lois."

Lois's only answer was a rippling laugh, as she mounted still higher up the broad oak staircase.

May continued her way along the hall till arrested by somebody with a rich baritone calling—

"Here, May, where are you off to with such a dignified bearing?"

"Oh! Durill, have you had a good day's sport?" and May went to him so gladly.

"Yes, pretty well, darling."

He drew her with him into his snuggery, a cosy room to the right of the hall, near the side door.

"What is the matter, May?" he asked, hold-her face between his hands.

"Nothing much; but Lois said you heard the carriage coming up; they are a long while getting to the top, are they not?"

Durill laughed.

"To tell the truth May, I drew on my imagination to get rid of Miss Lois. I did not hear the carriage; they won't be here for four minutes."

May smiled too. They were strikingly alike, this brother and sister.

May was the youngest, and Durill's pet. He

had chosen well; she had a true heart, and a sensible head. Durill used to nurse little big eyed May when a plump baby, and put her pink foot, with its five little toes, in his mouth.

And when questioned as to whose pet she was, and who she belonged to, she would lisp out, " Papa and Durill." She was Durill's right hand, helped him with his papers and letters, for the Squire left everything to Durill, and Durill in his turn left a good deal to May. She had her own side of the table, and her own chair in Durill's snuggery, and when their work was done they used to sit and chatter to each other; strange things they talked about sometimes, those two with their long heads. Durill used to learn from May, and May from Durill.

" What did you want to get quit of Lois for, Durill ?"

" Why she was harping on that old string again, those poor, unfortunate children, May, and I could not stand it. She seems to me to take a very unnatural view of the case. And she does not say a good say and have done with it, but she nibbles, nibbles; she is most tiresome."

"Yes, she is. Do you know it was she who made me out of temper just now. I met her at the bottom of the stairs, and she stopped to wish me joy because my rooms are next to those prepared for the poor little things; and if Crispin had been at home he would not have allowed it."

"Pray, what has Crispin to do with it?"

"Nothing that I can see; his rooms are not at our end, only near; and he can get moved further on if he does not like it, when he comes home."

"Of course he can. Such a selfish set. Julius won't mind, I am sure, any more than you and I will, May. I will never marry, May, if I am to have a wife like Lois, who is pretty enough, but dreadfully selfish."

" Durill, why don't you get married? You will be getting grey soon, and then no one will have you."

" Is that so? Well, then I will wait till I am grey to try my luck. But, May, I want to find a little girl like you; I want just such another wife as you will make."

May laughed.

" What a pity we are brother and sister, or we might have arranged matters to our satisfaction; you will make your old May conceited. But I am not thinking of getting married, Durill; what put it into your head?"

" Nothing particular, only I think I may return the compliment, and recommend you to be quick. You were twenty last week, and positively have no lover. I wonder how many Miss Lois has?"

" Ah! Lois; don't talk about it. The last time

she confided in me she had five, according to her own calculation."

" You don't say so ? Well, if she only hooks as decent a fellow as Mark Calvert she will do well."

" Have you seen him to-day ? How is Minnie ? The babies I need not ask about."

" Quite well, he said. He was going to Ash-worth to see someone who had been crushed in a thrashing machine. I met him by the Scrubbs."

" It is very nice having Minnie so close, but I must say I was not very sorry when Mark took her away, she was so like Lois."

" Right you are, May ; I like her better at a distance, too. I don't know how it is they are such lovely girls, and yet have such odd disposi-tions. Perhaps it is with being so much admired. Society is a bad thing for weak minds."

" I think so too, and I quite dread little Lucy

growing up, because Minnie will never be careful about such things, and the child will be quite ruined."

"Time enough for that, May; it is no use always looking for breakers ahead."

"Nay, I differ with you, Durill; we should be on the look out for breakers, and try to steer clear of them. Many a ship is lost because the watchman is asleep, and does not see the danger. 'Watch, lest ye enter into temptation.' We are all ships on the sea of life, and exposed to more dangers than those on the salt sea, yet no one watches, and some day we shall get on the rocks or in a whirlpool. Then we shall cry aloud like the disciples did during the storm, when Jesus was asleep. But he won't be in the boat with us, Durill."

"No, but he will be as near to us, little May."

They were silent for a few seconds, then there came the sound of carriage wheels.

" Here they are, Durill."

May opened the door.

There in the hall stood Miss Drever, holding two little children by the hands.

CHAPTER II.

" Oh, May, see love !"

" Yes, come in here, Judy, for a moment."

May drew the poor little things in, while Judith followed wearily, and, throwing back her veil, gazed at Durill and sighed.

" What is the matter, Judy ?"

" Oh, Durill ! you cannot think how bad things are with Gilbert. I dare not tell papa ; but I was so glad to bring these children away."

This caused Durill and May to look down more attentively at the two poor forlorn little creatures standing like outcasts, hand in hand ; a boy and a girl—twins—not quite four. The

boy, Ivo, was a manly little fellow with a proud
flash in his splendid eyes, infant though he was.
His hair was a dark chesnut, and curled naturally
down his back. He stood by his sister in a pro-
tecting sort of manner, which was truly touching
in one so young, while she, poor little darling,
crept closer to him, and buried her face in his
side. Her hair, like his, curled naturally, only it
was just a tone lighter. They were beautiful
children, without doubt; there was a good deal of
the wonderful beauty of Lois about them, which
was no wonder, for their father, Gilbert, was a
Benton Drever.

Little Evelyn began to cry—not a lusty roar, as
prognosticated by Aunt Lois, but silently, the
large drops rolling quickly over the fair round
cheeks, and the pretty mouth quivering. May
gathered her to her directly, and soothed her with
soft words and that beautiful tenderness which is
the inheritance of a true woman. There, held

closely, she gained courage, and raising her pretty head, called for Ivo to come. So May, with a smile, took him to her also, and commenced talking to them sweetly, making the poor little strangers feel at home. Great Durill looked on, a world of delight shining in his brown eyes, while Miss Drever seemed greatly relieved to be rid of them, and that they had taken to someone.

Judith Drever was thirty-one, a good strong woman, but she had had a blight when young, and it appeared to have dried up a great portion of the "milk of human kindness." She was kind-hearted, and did her duty, but she lacked gentleness. Her sorrow was not to be seen on her good-looking sensible face, it had worn away with the long long years, and at the same time worn away the sweetness of her youth. She felt for the griefs and troubles of others, but hers was a heavy hand to lay on an aching brow. Gilbert was her favourite, and to none had his life been a greater disappointment than to poor Judy. He had, like many others, taken the wrong turning. He was Madam's pet, because he was like her own family. Those who had the yellow locks and blue eyes stood a better chance with their lady mother, Madam Drever. She was a lovely woman, but of a worrying disposition and weak intellect. She had not the power to resist the pleading of her children when they asked for anything, even if it were bad for them. She winked at their faults, and screened them from the Squire, who, in his strong sense of honour, would have dealt severely with them. Thus it was that Gilbert, her third child, and the first like herself, went to ruin, on a gentlemanly scale. Indolence and vanity were the two first vices to shake him by the hand. He had wasted his time terribly. He imagined himself very clever, and boasted of what he could do ; but, as his brains might have been carried about in a thimble, they were soon used up, and then it became only too apparent to all beholders what sort of a young man Gilbert Benton Drever was.

He could not make anything for himself, though he had had every possible assistance rendered him, or if he did make it he lost it or spent it. So the post-bag contained no end of epistles, couched in the most flowery terms, and garnished with elaborate flourishes, the sum and substance of which was always, " I want some money." For the last few months these missives had been directed to either Madam or Judy, and they, woman like, strained every point to help their darling, always hoping he would turn over a new leaf, and quite unable to perceive that the scamp would sit still for ever with his mouth open for them or anyone else who was fool enough to feed him.

About five years before we became acquainted

with them he had taken to himself for better or for worse a young person of the name of Emily Ryde. He asked no one's opinion about it, for no better reason than that he knew his family would not agree to it.

So he married her and then informed his family of what he had done.

The Squire's face went purple as he read the letter, and then told the astonished family what their brother had accomplished.

The fruits of that ill-fated marriage were the two pretty little creatures we left on May's knee. Gilbert had coolly written to say that he and his wife were thinking of going abroad, and they could not take the children, therefore he asked for them a home till he was in a better position.

This request was strengthened by a letter to Durill from Julius, a rising barrister, living in the Temple, saying how Gilbert teased him, and what a life he was leading. Durill showed this epistle to their father, and the Squire determined to take the children. So that Tuesday morning Judy set off to fetch the neglected babies to the home ready for them at Wild Wood.

"Judy, have you seen mamma yet?"

"No, May, I have not, and I don't feel equal to just at present; you can't think how completely cut up I am. I don't wonder at Julius writing to you as he did, Durill. He was quite right in all he said, I only wish to goodness we had found it out sooner!" Judy was half crying while making this confession.

"What sort of a place was it, Judy, and what is she like?"

"*She!* don't mention it pray, Durill. Ah, such a creature, I can't think whatever Gilbert has been about; he must have been mad to have chained himself to such a girl. But I strongly suspect the great source of attraction was the few hundreds handed to her on her wedding day!"

"Good God! has Gilbert sunk so low as that?"

"Yes, indeed he has, Durill, and a great deal lower; he is lost, I plainly see, and no wonder either, with such a wife. Not that I want to excuse him, for my eyes are opened now. But there is no chance for him, even if he were disposed to make an effort, with such a drag."

"What is she like; good looking?"

"No. I don't consider her good looking, though no doubt many do. I can see no beauty in her. She is a vulgar, indolent, ignorant thing, with impudence enough for a dozen. I am certain you would both say the same if you saw her. She came to me this morning, and they did not know I was coming, you know, at half-past ten in a light silk dress, all daubed with grease, and her head ornamented with a green ribbon. She entered the room as upright as a grenadier guard, and swooped down upon me. I was petrified."

" How does she manage her house? What sort is it—a villa is it not ?"

" One of a row of small, but not bad houses. ' Terrogardo Villas,' or some such name. It is next to the end. But oh ! May, love, the dirt of the place ! I did not know where to sit down for the cleanest. And when I went upstairs I was obliged to wash the basin out before I could wash my hands."

" Poor Gilbert !" gesticulated May.

" Yes, you may well say *poor*, he is to be pitied; he looked to me ashamed. She actually spoke of the children as ' kids.' It is a blessing they are so young, they will forget what they have seen. If Gilbert had married a simple, modest, industrious girl, it would have been all right; she could have attended to the house and children. But that creature is not educated; all she does, if I may judge from the pile I saw in a corner, is to read ' Family Heralds.' She thinks too much of herself to see to the children or clean the house, and Gilbert has to have two dirty trolloping servants, when he is not in a position to pay one."

The babies Ivo and Evelyn had been playing with May's rings and staring about them; now, however, they turned round and faced Durill and Judy. So Durill took little Evelyn in his arms and kissed the rosy face. She stroked his face with her tiny hands, and was quite happy. "Say uncle Durill, little one." "Uncle Durill," lisped the child, for which she got nearly smothered with kisses. Suddenly the door opened, and in came Lois ready dressed for dinner.

"So you *are* back, Judy, I thought I saw a trunk going towards May's end of the house. And these are the children? What a pretty little trot. How sweet she would look in white and blue, eh, May? What is your name?"

But Evelyn did not seem to take to the cold lady bending over her, so she immediately buried her face on uncle Durill's broad chest, with a little whine of satisfaction. Durill gave her a fond hug, and laughed.

" You don't understand the infant age, Lois. They are too young to appreciate your pretty face or your ' get-up,' and you are too much afraid of having your yellow pyramid disarranged to bend to them. Try Ivo, he is of the male sex, perhaps he will not be indifferent to your charms."

Lois' pretty face flushed indignantly, and Judy and May could hardly refrain from laughing.

" Well, there's one thing to be said," answered the injured beauty, "if I don't understand them you do, but I don't believe it will last very long."

" Don't you? I would not prophecy any more were I you, Lois, considering how badly your first attempt in that line went off."

" What was that, pray ?"

" Why, that we should have a terrific outburst
the instant they set foot in the house.   They
have been here about a quarter of an hour and
we have not had it."

" Don't boast ; wait a bit, you will have it
presently.   You and your dear May have your
hands full."

" So it seems, for we sha'n't get any help from
you ; we don't expect it."

" Yes," said Judy, rising, " it does seem pretty
clear whose children they are going to be.   You
and May will divide the honours between you."

The elegant Lois was near the door, but she
condescendingly turned back to say—

" You people will all be late for dinner if you
don't make haste."

" Yes, I think we shall ; but it is an unusual
event, the arrival of two children.   Come, May,
you bring the little chap.   Is he too heavy for

you? If so give him to me, I can carry both easily."

"Oh! no, Durill, I can manage quite well; he is very light and I am very strong. But do move your great shoulders out of the way, I can't see where I am going to."

"If you don't behave yourself, Auntie May, I will carry the three of you off."

"Don't boast of your strength, you giant; you are quite equal to anything, I know. So, children, recollect whenever you want a nice ride you must go to Uncle Durill."

"Now, then, May, what is that you are putting into their young minds?"

"A ride on your back," said Ivo.

"Indeed! Well, we'll see. By the way, who is going to attend to these morsels?"

"Oh! Judy engaged Mrs. Cowley's sister, Parker, such a nice girl. She came last night, and I think she will do nicely."

"Well, here we are, so I must sit you down, darling. One sweet kiss for carrying you up-stairs."

Evelyn laughed, and readily kissed and patted the handsome face.

"Now, May, it is a case of be quick."

"Yes, but I must go and speak to nurse. Knock at my door as you pass, please, Durill."

"All right."

No one quite liked to mention the children to the Squire. Dessert was on the table, and they had told Parker to send them in. The old Squire was a kind-hearted man, but on the subject of Gilbert he was exceedingly bitter, and not with-out cause either. However long a purse may be, when there are perpetual draws upon it and a large family it all helps to shorten it.

May glanced at Judy to get her to name them, but Judy gave a decided shake of her sober head. Madam was busy talking to the beauty Lois about a journey to London, and a visit to Madame Elise, Regent Street.

" Yes, I think white trimmed with blue or pink, don't you, mamma? Minnie was talking about pale green, but I fancy white relieved with a colour this time, and moreover, it will be useful now we have that little Evelyn. That reminds me where are they? May, are they not to come in ?"

" Yes, I expect them every moment."

" That was a lucky stroke of Lois, eh, May ?" whispered Durill. " The most useful thing she has done for many a day."

The Squire looked up.

" Ah ! where are the children, May ?"

" Coming, papa; I told Parker, but perhaps they are too sleepy after their journey."

" Judy, did you see Gilbert ?"

" Yes, papa, I did; also his wife."

This was said in the most uncompromising

tone possible. Every one was silent. It was quite evident the Squire would have to ask if he intended to be enlightened; Judy would volunteer nothing. The silence was rather embarrassing.

"Lois, sherry?"

"Please, mamma."

Miss Lois never seemed to feel anything. She was indifferent to other people's troubles, and never had any of her own. Happy Lois! Yes, in one sense, but not in another. When trouble came to her she would have to seek shelter, she had none within herself. Like all butterflies, her place was in the sunshine.

"Judy," continued the Squire, "what do you think of Gilbert?"

"Nothing," replied that lady, after a pause.

"Judy, my dear," interposed madam, softly, while she fidgeted her bracelets nervously.

"No, no, Jeanie," called out the Squire to his

wife, " no more blinds, if you please ; I have had enough of them. The time for concealment is past. Speak, Judith, my daughter, what do you think Gilbert is doing ?"

" He is not doing anything, papa," answered Judy, raising her calm face, " and what is worse, he does not try to do anything."

" Do you mean to tell me he does not attend to his business ?"

" He has no business; his office has been closed for some time. He says he could get no work."

" Then upon what is he living ?"

" On what you allow him, and what he can screw out of Julius, and for the rest he goes into debt. I fear he will never do any good again, and the wife he has chosen is not at all calculated to spur him on."

A dead silence followed this confession of

Judy's; even the gay Lois was awed. May and
Durill exchanged glances; they knew what it cost
poor brave Judy to tell of her favourite brother.
But she would be true to her father, even at the
expense of her own feelings. She had dreaded
being asked, because, as she told May—

"I must tell the truth."

"Judy, I am entirely of your opinion on the
subject. I don't believe he ever will do any good.
I told your mother so six years ago. Now, however, the doubt is settled, I will not help those
who will not help themselves. I firmly believe
had I refused assistance at the onset, he would
have exerted himself. If he had been the son of
a poor man, he would have had to either work or
starve—and hunger is a capital stimulant. But
from this quarter I stop my allowance; it falls
due on the 29th—eh, Durill?"

"Yes, sir."

" Well, then, he gets no more after that. He shall not be helped on his way to the devil by me. I have taken the children, and he and his wife must look out for themselves. As it is, he has had considerably over his share, and that before my death, too."

Madam commenced to use her lace handker- chief, but not without an eye to effect, while her blue eyes shot quick lightning at Judy. It had considerably astonished Madam Drever to hear Judy take sides against Gilbert, whom she had hitherto helped to screen. But there is a limit to all things, and amongst the rest Judy's patience.

The visit to Terrogardo Villas had revealed a great deal to Judy, which in all probability but for that visit they would never have found out. For shocking to state, Gilbert did not tell the truth ; Julius had been the first to see round the curtain, and he had written very strongly on the subject to Durill.   But he did not go to Red Hill; he merely drew his own conclusion from what Gilbert told him, so the blow had in reality fallen upon Judy.

CHAPTER III.

"It is a quarter-past seven ; I wonder whether those children are coming, May?" asked the Squire.

"I don't know what is keeping them, I am sure ; shall I go and see ?"

May rose, but before she reached the door there was a knock, and it opened.

There stood Parker with Ivo and Evelyn, looking charming in pretty white frocks. Everyone was surprised ; they were wonderfully lovely children. They came straight to May and Durill. The old Squire put up his glass, and exclaimed "Bless me !" while genuine tears ran down madam's cheeks this time. May led them to the

Squire, and they gazed at him fearlessly, and put their little fat hands on his knees.

Parker had vanished, or she might have been surprised to see the almost vicious manner in which the Squire kissed the little things. They were fearless, happy children, and they went round the table first to one and then another, getting nice things. But they found their resting places: Evelyn on Uncle Durill's knee, and Ivo on Aunt May's.

" I thought they were Gilbert's babies, Durill ?" said the Squire.

" So I believe they are, sir," answered Durill, laughing ; " but they seemed to take to May and me the moment they came, and I think we are very glad to have it so, eh, May ?"

" Oh ! yes, certainly ; they will be quite playthings for us, and prevent us getting either selfish or bad tempered. Papa, I wish you would give me one of those oranges for Ivo."

" Certainly ; here, little man. And what must grandpapa give you, my little maid ?"

" 'Ponge cake," replied Miss Evelyn, wriggling with delight on Durill's knee, and extending two little fat fists, each armed with a " 'ponge cake," across the table.

" Durill," called Lois, " I should advise you to give your child a drink of water ; the rate she is cramming those dry cakes down is dangerous I am sure."

" You don't say so. Judy, that goblet, please. May, do you see any alarming symptoms ? do you recommend patting her on the back or shaking her ?"

" Nonsense, Durill, the child is not going to choke ; she is all right, dear little thing."

" Then, ' dear little thing,' turn round, and let me look at you."

Evelyn rolled her little hot body round, smothering the plate with her balloon petticoats, and commenced a furious attack of kissing, smearing her uncle's face all over. But he stood it all like a Spartan, indeed he seemed rather to like it if one might judge by the number of squeezes her plump little body received. She talked and jabbered away in his face, much to the amusement of the Squire, who at last found voice to exclaim—

"I had no idea you were so fond of children, Durill."

"Had you not? Well, certainly you have never had an opportunity of judging, for Minnie's babies are rather too small to play with at present, though I had a grand romp with Lucy the other day."

"By-the-bye, that reminds me," said madam, "how is Arnold getting on? There was some trouble about his teeth; Minnie told me Mark was afraid of convulsions."

"Well, I don't know; I did not hear anything about it, and he looked all right. He stuffed everything into his mouth that he could lay hands on, and I suppose that is a sign of teeth."

"Evelyn, where did you get that pretty frock from ?" asked Lois, who, as usual, had an eye to the finery.

The child looked at Lois, but never uttered a sound.

"Tell Aunty Lois, Evelyn," whispered Durill.

Instantly the little girl glanced at him, and said quite loud—

"I don't know."

She was evidently puzzled herself.

"Ivo, do you know ?" asked madam.

"No, grandmamma ; they are new."

"Well, perhaps Judy can solve the riddle."

"Yes I can, Lois. I got them along with a number of other things this morning at Sill's. The rest are to be sent on to-night, they required several alterations. The clothes they had were

not new, and I could not let them come with
them alone."

"No, you did quite right, Judy. Since we are
to have the children they must rank with us, and
be dressed according to their position. Though
I daresay your mamma can find plenty of things
for them."

"I am not so sure of that, my dear. Minnie
took all my treasures for Lucy, but no doubt we
shall manage very well. May, you must have a
hunt amongst your possessions."

"Willingly; but I imagine Lois is the best
person to apply to for choice bits, I never purchase too much material."

"Oh! I must say I like that; so I am to dress
these two little creatures?"

"No, most certainly not; I don't mean anything of the kind, which you know perfectly well,
only if you have any pieces suitable, I shall be

glad of them. Ivo must be put into nickerbockers soon ; don't you think so, Judy ?"

" Yes, and I have some capital stuff for that purpose."

" Here's Parker ; I wonder who she has come for ?"

" Oh ! is it time, Aunty May ?"

" Yes, Ivo dear ; you will never be able to get up in the morning if you don't go to bed. Go and say good-night to grandpapa and all round."

Ivo made a tour of the table, but Evelyn never offered to move. She sat still, with her plump arms clasped round Durill's neck, and her cheek pressed against his, looking defiance at Parker through a shower of curls. Durill smiled.

" Come, Evelyn, Ivo has kissed everyone, and you are not off my knee yet."

She shuffled down, thereby twisting her petti-coats nearly round her neck, and ran off to kiss " Good-night." Parker and Ivo stood waiting at the door, but she darted past them round the other end, and arrived puffing at Durill's side. He looked down from his superior height, at the small creature whose fat fingers were doing a faint scrape on his leg.

" Why you don't mean to say you are not gone ?"

" I go wid you !"

" With me ? but I am not going to bed; my half-past-seven go to bed days ended long ago."

" The truth is, she wants you to carry her up those long stairs, Durill ; she is young, and I am old, so I can feel for her, and it is a tremendous pull up. That's it, is it not, Evelyn ? you want Uncle Durill to carry you up to bed this once ?"

" Ris, grandpapa."

" You mean this twice, papa," said Lois ; " that is the consequence of beginning a bad practice, Durill."

" You quite astonish me, Aunt Lois, I had no idea you were so prudent or farseeing. But I am not so sure about its being a bad practice. Come along little one, your horse is ready."

" Who is your horse, Ivo ?'

" Aunty May, grandpapa."

" Aunty May! is he not too heavy for you, May, my dear ?"

" No, papa, I can carry him perfectly well. See, Ivo ; mount that chair. There, now, off we go."

Parker followed with one of Miss Evelyn's shoes, which had slipped off in her exertions to drive her " Gee-gee. "

The babies were carried up and deposited in their nursery safely. May was quite flushed with the pace they had come at.

" Capital exercise, this, May," laughed strong Durill, who, to use a horsey phrase, had " not turned a hair."

" Yes, indeed, I don't think I shall ever require to embrace 'Banting' while these little tyrants remain."

"To bed, to bed, you sleepy head."

" Good-night, darlings ; be good children."

" May, I want to say something to you, let us stand here, there is no one about. I had a letter this morning from Crispin, and he wants some money at once."

"Money, Durill ? impossible, why it is not three weeks since he had his allowance, and that nearly double, too."

" Well, he says he wants some badly. I fancy he is in some scrape, but I don't know how to tell my father."

" Nor I, because his allowance is so handsome, and he has nothing to pay out of it. Really, Durill, I by chance got hold of his last year's college bills the other morning, and I assure you I was shocked. He is far more extravagant than

Julius was. It is awfully expensive; I hope he is not idling his time away. But I am afraid he is going to follow Gilbert's example."

"Never, surely; one in a family is quite enough, May. But I must confess I don't like or understand him continually wanting money. And I don't see where it is to come from just at present. Because everything is settled, and the Squire is full of those new cottages. He will not have anything out of order in his affairs; he puts down a certain sum for everything, and he is very liberal, too; but he will not have it overdrawn, unless there is some excellent cause."

"Well, what is to be done, Durill? If Crispin really requires the money, I suppose he must have it some way, or else he will resort to some underhanded scheme that will prove twice as expensive in the long run. Go to the Jews, or get money advanced on his prospects. He is a Benton

Drever, Durill, and up to all manner of dodges. I wonder why he does not apply to his mother. She might part with her grandmother's diamonds to oblige him."

"You are speaking bitterly, May. Our mother is a foolish woman; but we must bear with all and everything, because she is our mother."

"Yes, I know that perfectly well; but, still, I cannot help feeling annoyed, for papa has to pay for her ridiculous pampering and favouritism, and Cris is just putting his feet in Gilbert's marks. Julius never caused any trouble, and look how industrious and clever he is! Moreover, I question whether Crispin is really benefitting very much by his prolonged stay. He ought to have passed last term; he was well drilled by Dr. Tinley."

"Yes, you are correct, he should have gone up last term, and it annoyed my father extremely.

But the question just now is, where is this money to come from ?"

" How much is it ?"

" Well, he very coolly asks for as much over a hundred as I can send, but certainly not less than a hundred."

" Good gracious, Durill! He must have got into some scrape or other."

" So I think, May, and I have almost made up my mind not to name it to the Squire; it will put him so much out of the way, especially now that Gilbert has shown up in his true colours."

" Then what are you going to do?"

" Why, I am going to send him one hundred, and not a penny over, and a stiff letter, telling him it will be the last he will get from me."

" You are a good fellow, Durill; I wonder what we should do without you? You spend a great deal of money on first one thing and then another."

" Well, I can afford it ; my engineering pays well. I have made a great deal out of that new boiler, May. And Howards want me to sell it to them, but that I won't do, because it pays better to keep the right. That reminds me I want your assistance in the morning, if you can spare time, May."

" Oh, yes, quite easily; I have nothing to do particularly. What do you want me for ?"

" To help with a new plan, and write me the descriptive letters ; also to overlook the cottage plans again. Jones tells me our idea will cost over the stated sum to carry out. So we must reduce it."

" I am sorry for that, because we only gave just what would render them comfortable."

Durill smiled.

" What about the pet schemes to induce them to be neat and orderly, eh, May ?"

" Well, yes, that certainly necessitates the expenditure of more money; but then how can a poor woman with a large family keep her house tidy and clean with so few apartments, small windows, and no water in the house? One pump to supply six cottages. And then, see the evil consequences of that pump! Three, perhaps, go at the same time to draw water, and there they stand gossiping, while the baby sets fire to its clothes, or the child left in charge of it drops it into a pail of hot water, which has been heated in a pan because there is no boiler. Then, again, they have no gardens, half of them. Look at Mr. Chaters, for instance; not a scrap. So when the poor men come home they cannot remain in the hot stuffed cottage, when the children, being put to bed, are at concert pitch; they have no nice little plot of ground to take their attention, so the result is they go to the public-house. I am certain the builders of cottages will be held responsible for one half the misery and sin in them."

" But our village is not like that, May ?"

" No, of course it is not; but still it might be improved. There are many little comforts they might have, which I am sure the poor things would appreciate."

" Well, May, perhaps some day we shall see you a ' Lady Bountiful.' "

" No, never, for I shall never have money enough, and no great man would marry me because I am not good looking enough to suit them. I am going to remain Miss Drever, the old maid."

" Indeed, you will be obliged to dispose of Judy first."

" Who is taking my name in vain ?" asked Miss Drever, coming softly behind them.

" Oh! it is you, Judy! Well, Durill is thinking of a plan to get rid of you, that is all."

" Get rid of me ! why, what for ?"

" So that May, here, may be the ' old maid' of the family. That is the height of her ambition ; and she has called me to her assistance."

May burst out laughing.

" Durill is only cramming, Judy. But the conversation did get upon that topic, and Durill asked me how I was going to dispose of you after hearing my desire."

Judy smiled.

" You will find it a difficult task, May. You had better put a board up in the village—' For sale, that young woman, Judith Drever, warranted sound in everything but her temper. Applications to be made at Wild Wood.' "

" Yes, and the house would be full, Judy. There would be Mr. What's-his-name? the widower with seven children."

" Stop, for goodness sake, May, my ambition does not extend that far."

" Poor Judy," laughed Durill, " but we have been here long enough, it seems to me ; suppose we find a seat?"

" Why, what have you two been talking about?"

" Laying plans to blow you all up to-night, Judy."

" Ah ! then all I have to do is to run down stairs and inform against you."

" Run, make haste ; May and I have still got plenty to say."

" And I am not to know? Well, I don't care as long as it is only your own business, because you are two wise ones, but I am always fearful of the rest."

" Never mind, Judy ; Gilbert, may be, will take a better turn."

" Never, Durill, while his wife lives. I pray that the rest of you may remain single for ever rather than marry such a creature."

" Come, let us go down; Judy, are you not coming ?"

" No, May, not at present; the children are asleep by now, of course ?"

" Oh, yes, it is some time since they went to bed, dear little trots."

" May, I am going to the stables for a short time," said Durill, when they reached the hall. " What are you going to do ?"

" I don't know ; write love letters, I think. But don't stay long, Durill, the tea tastes nasty when you are away."

" Does it? you lovely little May ! Now, if you will wait in our snuggery for me I will be all the quicker."

" Yes, I will wait for you or follow you."

May settled herself comfortably, and commenced writing at express speed. Hers was an extensive correspondence, and she, unlike most young ladies, attended to it regularly.

" Good little May," exclaimed Durill, who shortly after came in. " Do you know Floss has such a pretty family, all white like herself?"

" Has she? Did you bring one for me to see ?"

" Bless me, no ; you surely don't think I am as mad about puppies and kittens as you are ?"

" Come, Mr. Durill, you know you are very fond of them ; are you sure you have not got one in your back pocket ?"

" Yes, quite sure, love. Have you finished your letters ?"

" Not all, but it does not signify, because the mail does not go out till the 23rd, and I shall have plenty of time before then."

" May, I have got a fancy in my head—I don't know whether there is any cause for it or not, but I imagine Lois is setting her cap at Captain Hardwick."

" Captain Hardwick! I don't know, Durill; she may be; perhaps he is setting his at her?"

" No, that he is not, I am certain; but, to tell the truth, I dread any of your hopeless attachments. Judy has never been the same since that luckless affair. She puts me in mind of a cup of strong tea without sugar."

" Yes, Judy never has been quite the same since; it was an awful pity. I remember papa's finding it out, young as I was; and, moreover, I always suspected Gilbert had a hand in that business."

" So did I; and it seemed very likely, too, for he was Gilbert's friend."

" I wonder what he is doing? he was handsome enough for anything. Do you recollect him singing the 'Village Blacksmith' that eventful night?"

" Perfectly, and I can guess what he is about. He was sent abroad because his family were ashamed of him, and also for a little shuffling, so no doubt he is living on his wits somewhere."

" I don't know what ever Judy saw in him. He was good-looking to be sure, but to me there was something wanting in his face."

" It was a sort of infatuation, and truly he was a very amusing, jolly fellow, but he would never have done for Judy's husband—he was penniless, or next door to it then, and when the governor found it out, wasn't he wild though?"

" Yes—poor Judy ! Shall we go to the drawing-room, Durill ?"

" Yes, Aunt May."

CHAPTER IV.

" THANK goodness, Crispin comes home to-
morrow !" exclaimed Lois, one morning at breakfast. "I wonder what his friend Ted Archer will
be like? I hope he is a nice fellow;—we do so
want a few agreeable, jolly men in this place.
Don't you think we might have a dance this
Christmas, mamma?"

"A ball, Lois? Ah, my love, it makes such
an upset. We shall have dinner and evening
parties, of course, but a dance is really an under-
taking; but we will see."

" Why, there is Judy; she and Mrs. Morrison
can see to everything for you, mamma."

"As you are so anxious to have a ball, Lois, supposing you assist Morrison, I don't believe we, any of us, care for it but you."

"Now, Judy you are wrong for once, because it was Minnie who first put it into my head, and I am certain Crispin would enjoy it. Really, I have a most thankless office: I have to propose everything, and receive black looks and temper for my pains. I told Minnie how it would be."

"You and Minnie are like a couple of gnats—always worrying after something, Lois."

"Well, papa, it is hard that we merry ones can never have any pleasure, all because Durill, Judy, May, and Julius are of a serious turn of mind."

"Come, Lois, don't pout; no one said you might not have your much-wished-for party; as for Durill and May, they have not said a word yet, and Julius is not present."

"Then we may have it, papa?"

"Not so fast, my dear, not so fast; I did not

say you might have it, because, as your mamma just now told you, it makes a great upset, and we are neither of us so young as we used to be. Quieter parties are more suited to my taste, but it is for you and your mamma to settle."

" Lois, I am sure you won't press it, since you hear that papa does not desire it ?"

" It would not be much use, May, with you all against me."

" I forgot to tell you, sir, that I went about that donkey for the children, and Bland wants two pounds for it."

" Two pounds ! Well, is it worth it, Durill, because the children must have something to ride on ; and Parker will do better with a donkey than a pony. Moreover, I will not have anything but good horseflesh in my stables, and, then, sometimes those well-bred ponies are skittish, and require a man to lead them."

" Yes, that is perfectly true ;—it was in that

way that Mr. Shutt's boy was crippled for life. They put him on a dashing pony, the prettiest thing I ever saw, and sent him out with the nurse. Something or other frightened it; the nursemaid got alarmed and let go. The pony raced off, threw poor Harry, and injured his spine. Shutt was only telling me about it the last time I was over there."

" Dear me—how sad! Poor boy! Well, Durill, we will have this quiet donkey, and see that the saddle is nice and easy. A pad, had it not better be?"

"Yes, I think so; and they are making a sort of chair, or, rather, two chairs for children now, so that two can ride together. That, I imagine, would suit Ivo and Evelyn?"

"Very likely. See after it to-day, Durill; it will be a nice Christmas present for them."

" Yes, I will; I shall be over there this morning."

Next day Crispin arrived with his friend Mr. Edward Archer, called Ted for short—a good-looking, merry fellow, with a great deal to say for himself. He and Lois seemed intent upon captivating each other, and, really, Lois could be agreeable enough when it suited her—all smiles and graces.

"What do you think of him, May?" asked Durill.

"He is very nice, and decidedly good-looking; but to tell the candid truth, I dread another Charles Blackett performance. Those things always annoy me immensely, Durill. I am like papa for that—I detest a flirt. Lois is, I think, worse than Minnie was, and trouble enough there used to be over her flirtations."

"Why, May, you little darling, nearly every girl flirts."

"Yes, I suppose they do, but that does not make it any better, that I can see. It is just acting lies instead of speaking them, Durill, and they will be recorded just the same. Besides, there is no necessity for them; flirting is not essential to one's happiness. It is simply an idle, loose amusement, which must be disgusting to any sensible, honourable man, because there is so much hypocrisy required to carry it off. I feel very strongly on that subject, it seems to me lowering; in my eyes the girl who flirts loses caste, and it wounds me to think that one bearing the name of Frever should stoop to such a degrading pastime."

"But, May, how about the men? They are quite as bad as the women."

"Not quite, Durill, and moreover, if a lady will not flirt a gentleman will respect her all the more. There are exceptions to the rule, I am aware, but what true-hearted woman—a lady in mind—wants the love or admiration of a scoundrel? If the women stopped flirting the men would, and we should very soon have our drawing-rooms clear of heartless, brainless puppies."

" Well said, May. We men do take our cue from the ladies, because they are supposed to be ' true of heart ' and ' pure of mind,' and I agree with you, there is something very repulsive in a flirt. I do not know a more pitiable sight than a young girl flirting."

" And we get your pity, then ? It almost makes me blush. I often wondered what Charles Blackett thought of Lois. She carried on most shamefully with that young man. I hope he will never come down here again."

" Did you never take her to task about it, May ?"

" Many a time. We used to have such battles over it. But at last he wrote to papa, actually asking for his consent when he got that living in Stafford somewhere, and papa sent for Lois to explain it to him. Then it all came out. Lois had not the least intention of marrying the poor fellow—never had. She had done it all by way of a joke, and for want of something better to do, I expect. Papa was so wrath. I was in his study at the time. He frightened Lois dreadfully. He told her he would make her marry him since she had gone so far. So Lois commenced to cry, like mamma, with her lace handkerchief, but her tears had no effect upon papa, so, as a last resource, she fell headlong off her chair in a dead faint, but managed not to strike her head in falling."

" And the Squire was beaten, of course ?"

" Yes, it was no use talking any more, with her full length on the floor. There was some water on the table, and he dashed it all over her, but never offered to lift her up. When Lois thought she had been long enough on her back, she came to with several gasps, and walked out with a dropping head. But I don't think I ever saw papa so angry. He blamed mamma for a great deal of it."

"What for ?"

"Why, he thought mamma ought to have seen how things were going on, and in truth she did see, only it was Lois, so she never interfered. But the worst of it was, papa charged me that if ever I knew of anything of the kind again I was to inform him immediately."

"By Jove ! the old gentleman must have been up. Does Lois know of that ?"

"Of course not, and that is what renders me so uncomfortable with regard to this Mr. Archer. He has been in the house four days, and according to my idea, things have gone quite far enough already. But perhaps I am too straight laced. Any way, I shall not tell at present, and not at all if I can possibly help it. It is no pleasant thing to have to tell of one's sister."

"No, that it is not, but it is better than letting

her do the same again.   If she were my daughter I should shake her well."

"Yes, I almost think it would require a shake to arouse Lois. She knows she is safe with mamma, and she does not suspect that papa will ever find anything out. And then, as she said to me the last time I remonstrated with her—

"'It is what every young lady does, May.'

"'That may be correct enough, but then they are not the daughters of John Reginald Drever.'"

"Well, it is as Judy says, a nuisance, to have such family troubles. By-the-bye, I named to Crispin about that hundred pounds, and he took it quite coolly, and all I could get out of him was, 'My honour was at stake.' So I suppose I am to find money to keep his 'honour' in the right place. But he has got the last, and I told him so. I am loth to confess it, but really I see a wonderful change in Crispin, he appears to me perfectly hardened and indifferent. And I am beginning to echo your forebodings that he is copying from Gilbert."

" Ah, Durill, I am afraid you are right, I cannot make him out, and he is so uncertain in his temper, especially with the children, and a bad temper with children is complete ruin for them. Moreover, Ivo and Evelyn are particularly sweet and tractable little things. But just to show you how shrewd you are, I will relate to you what took place no later than last night. They pray for everyone they love, little darlings, before I lift them into bed, and I had noticed previously that they left Lois out when they could. So now that Crispin is home, and they have had many opportunities of learning to love him, I told Ivo to include uncle Crispin. The child stopped short and looked at me. ' Well, what is it, Ivo ?'

" ' Aunty May, I cannot say that.'

" ' Why not, dear ?'

" ' Because I *don't* love uncle Crispin, he does not love me and Evelyn.'

" ' Yes he does, Ivo.'

" ' He told me to go away and not tease him, and he would not crack me any nuts.'

" ' And did you get nothing ? '

" ' No, Aunty May, I did not like to move, and go round the table.' "

" Now, Durill, you see the little fellow was wounded, hurt, because Crispin would not crack him any nuts. He saw at once that Crispin did not care about him, and he could not say he loved him. He is too young at present to know any-thing about the love due to all mankind. He loves those who are kind and tender to him, and his honest little baby heart would not allow him to say ' I love uncle Crispin.' He recollected the uncracked nuts. So Crispin, by his selfishness, has lost the love of a little child, and Christ loved little children."

"May, what did you say to Ivo. Did you compel him to say it?"

"Compel him! compel him to go contrary to his conscience, and play the hypocrite? Certainly not, Durill. Crispin would have been no better for that. God listens to little children, and a prayer from their pure little minds is of great value. They are much nearer to Him than we are, by reason of their purity. They know no sins or wretchedness, their souls are without a blot. To see those babies clasp their little hands, and ask our Father to bless us, each named separately, in all the earnestness of their minds, is a thing to be remembered. Oh! Durill, it is a foolish man or woman that discards the love of one of Christ's little ones."

"I shall come into the nursery to hear you

teach the children, May. I have missed the last few days, but I am in want of teaching myself."

"But I don't think I can teach you anything, Durill. Indeed, many times the children teach me."

CHAPTER V.

" Mrs. Calvert," announced Blake.

" Minnie, darling, how do you do ?"

" Pretty well, only mamma, I am *so* worried."

" What with, dear ?   Let me take your hat off, and jacket, there—you will be more comfortable now.   Tell me what your trouble is ?"

" Trouble ! oh, dear ! why the children, they are both ill, and Mark is *so* unfeeling, he says perhaps Arnold will die."

" And Minnie, you have left him to the care of Janet," exclaimed Judy, who had just entered.

" Dear me, Judy, don't look so astonished ; if you had been chained up as I have during the last two days, I think you would have come out. And I want to see Lois about a bonnet, I am undecided what to get. What do you recommend, mamma, fawn, or one in the new shade? It would suit my hair nicely, I fancy, only it might become common in the village."

"Minnie, I really think you might dispense with a bonnet at present; if little Arnold dies you cannot wear fawn or the new shade."

"Oh, Judy! how unkind you are to say such a thing to me, his mother. You have no feeling."

Pretty Minnie Calvert commenced to cry and sob, Judy looking on, her proud lip curling with scorn.

"I wonder how you can be so absurd, Minnie. You say yourself that the child is seriously ill, and yet you leave him and want advice about a new bonnet. Yet when I suggest that he may die you commence to cry. It is extremely inconsistent, Minnie."

" If I had known I was to have such a reception I would never have come, I can assure you ; but it is hard if one cannot come to one's own in one's trouble."

" Judy, I am astonished. Don't you see Minnie is quite unnerved with so much anxiety ?"

" Is she. Well, I am sorry I am so dull at comprehension. I had better leave you to console her, mamma."

" Judy is very hard, don't you think so, mamma ?"

" Well, my love, she is quite a Drever, not in the least like my family. Have you seen Crispin's friend, Mr. Archer ?"

" No, not yet, but Lois has told me a great deal about him ; she appears quite smitten."

" Indeed ! well, he is too. But really that is no wonder, for she is a particularly sweet girl. I must contrive some parties, but the Squire is so averse to anything of the kind. Lois quite pines for a little gaiety, dear girl, and I fully intended sending her up to town to your Aunt Sophia, but that again your papa objects to."

" Yes, it would be a good thing to send Lois and May up, though I don't fancy she would take. But she does really manage Ivo and Evelyn capitally. Mark is always singing her praises to me, and he hinted that perhaps she would come and nurse Lucy and Arnold through this sickness. It really would be a great relief to me. I am so nervous, I cannot endure the least sound or the least exertion. I think I must take after your family, dear mamma."

" You do, my love, Lois and you. The Ladies Benton are noted for particularly delicate nerves. Yes, it certainly would be a great point gained to have May at hand, she is so wonderfully strong— quite a Drever. But I question whether your papa or Durill will spare her; she belongs to them."

" Oh ! I know Durill thinks there is no one

like May. Mark has pretty much the same opinion too. But I will try, at all events."

While this conversation had been going on before the fire in Madam's room, Judy had sought May, and found her, as usual, busy with Durill. Both were intent over some parchment, but raised their heads at her entrance.

" Want me, Judy ; anything the matter with the children ?"

" No, May, nothing is to do with our children, but something is amiss with Minnie's."

" Why, what ?"

" That I cannot rightly say, for Minnie is rather misty in her statements. But I went into mamma's room just now to speak to her about Sharp's wife, who wants help, and who should I find there but Minnie, looking charming in an elegant costume, irreproachably put on, and, according to her own account, overwhelmed with grief."

"It seems to me that you are rather misty, Judy. Don't lose the place, May dear. Go on, Judy; what calamity has befallen Mrs. Minnie?"

"Oh, Durill, don't laugh; I really am serious. She says the children are both very ill, and Mark fears poor little Arnold will die, and yet she leaves them to the mercy of Janet, and comes up here to see mamma, and consult Lois about a new bonnet. I was so much astonished that I could not help exclaiming, and I got called un-feeling and cruel because I did not see that dear Minnie was quite overdone, &c., &c."

"Do you really mean that, Judy?"

"Yes, indeed, I do, Durill; I am perfectly dis-gusted. I think I shall go down and see the poor little things. Will you come, May?"

"I don't know, Judy; it depends upon what it is. We must not forget Ivo and Evelyn, they would easily catch any complaint."

"Very true, May. So Judy shall go alone,

and you will stay and look after the children. Minnie wants boxing. I really wonder how Mark has patience with her."

"They took each other for better or worse, Durill, and Minnie is a sweet little creature."

"So she is, when everything goes the right way; but just wait, if Mark lost his practice, or got anything amiss with him she would consider herself very badly dealt with, and sit and wring her pretty hands and cry. That is not the sort of wife for my money, Judy!"

"Your money! Wait till you get in love, and then talk."

"Now, May, you have lost the place, though I asked you not."

"No, indeed, I have not. There's someone at the door; come in."

"Please, Miss May, Madam wants you in her room."

"Very well, say I am coming, Blake."

"May, I should not be a bit surprised if they want you to nurse these babies."

"Well, then she sha'n't, Judy, so that is the long and short about it. Stop a minute, May, I am coming with you. See, I have put the plan into the bill-drawer till we come back."

"You come too, Judy?"

"No, thank you, May; I shall get the credit of putting you up to saying no as it is."

"May, look here; I shall not let you go, if that is what they want, so you need not say one word."

"But, Durill, if she—"

"Hush!"

"How are you, Minnie? How is Mark and the babies?"

"They are ill, Durill, and I am so anxious."

"Indeed! I should not have thought so!"

"What is the matter with them, Minnie?"

"Colds, May, and slight inflammation. Mark

is very fearful for Arnold. If anything happened to him, I believe it would kill me. May, why don't you dress your hair in the new style? Lois would show you, I am sure, or I will."

Durill and May exchanged glances.

"Thank you, Minnie; but I think this way will do very well. It is very comfortable, and does not take long."

"I am afraid you are becoming careless, May; mamma, don't you think so? It used not to be so when I was at home. Lois should take my place; I must speak to her about it."

Durill fidgetted on the table, and May's cheeks burnt.

"I recommend you to leave things alone, Minnie. They are very much better as they are. Lois cannot teach May anything."

"Really, Durill, you are ridiculous; you will have two old maids on your hands. Judy and

May will never marry, I am sure, if they go on so absurdly."

"Is that your opinion? I differ from you, Minnie. I think they have a grand sight better chance than Lois, who, by the way, is roaming about the woods with Archer. Mother, I consider that improper, and I hope you will stop it. It is not in accordance with Lois's position. If she cannot see those things for herself it is your place to. The Squire would be wild if he knew."

"I did not know Lois was out, Durill."

"Well, she is; I saw her go more than two hours since down to the 'Druid's Walk.' She will be the talk of the village shortly."

"But Crispin is with them."

"No he is not. Crispin has ridden over to Middleton's about a pointer they have for sale."

"Mr. Archer is a very nice young man, I am

sure, Durill. His uncle is Lord Farrington, and his father is Sir Stockwell Archer."

" I don't care if his father is a king, it does not make it any better, the fact still remains the same. Lois Benton Drever is flirting in anything but a lady-like manner with him."

"Then in that case it would be a desirable match for dear Lois, mamma."

" Whatever are you talking about, Minnie? No one is contemplating marriage. Who knows what his family are? His mother may have been somebody's cook. He may be a scoundrel himself for anything we know to the contrary."

" Why, he is Crispin's friend, Durill ?"

" I know that ; so was Norton Gilbert's friend, and look what came of that."

" But that was Judy's fault, Durill. No one asked her to fall in love with him."

" And no one asked him to fall in love with her, Minnie. It was poor Judy's misfortune, not her fault. He was a nice enough fellow, but a mere adventurer; he had not a penny, and his family had cast him off for misconduct. Yet he was of good family, and came here as Gilbert's friend. No, I thank you, we will have no more of that; Lois has not got the sense of Judy, and could not be brought to reason. It is a pity though, if every fellow is to be analysed before he is introduced, all because of a flirty little girl."

" Yes, I really think I will speak to Lois about it. But, May, Minnie wants you to go and help her with the children for a few days."

" Have you no nurse, Minnie?"

" Oh, yes, Durill, we have Janet; I should never be able to get along without her."

" Then I don't see that you want May; we have two children here and not a very experienced nurse."

" But there is Nurse Joyce, she might go, I am sure, mamma?"

" Yes, certainly, old nurse has nothing to do? you can have her, Minnie."

This was evidently not quite what Minnie wanted. But big Durill looked stern, and determined not to part with May.

" Thank you, mamma, but I really should prefer May, because there is a dinner party at the Rectory, and I wanted to go to town and see the newest things. Have you had any invitations here, May ?"

" Yes, as usual, all are invited; but, of course, are not going. Durill won't go, and I won't, and I don't fancy Judy will, but Crispin and Lois intend to."

" I daresay you would prefer May, Minnie, but I cannot spare her; besides, old nurse has had no end of experience, and surely she and Janet can manage. If not, you will be obliged to forego your parties, Minnie, that is all."

"That I don't agree to. Mark does not want to

go, but then, perhaps, he may alter his mind, and a doctor's wife is generally obliged to go alone, and say her husband is busy. So there is nothing to prevent me."

"Then since all is satisfactorily arranged, I will wish you good bye, Minnie. Tell Mark I will drop in and have a look at him soon, perhaps to-night."

Durill left the room, and almost immediately Blake again appeared, with a highly-amused twinkle in his eye, and said—

" Miss May, you are wanted."

Minnie was in the midst of an eloquent appeal to May, " how free she would be, and how easy in her mind, if May was there to overlook Janet while the children were poorly, and then they were so fond of Aunty May."

The sudden appearance of Blake stopped Minnie, and May, with a hurried " excuse me," escaped.

" Who wants me, Blake, papa?"

" No, Miss May, not the Squire, Mr. Durill sent me in."

By this time the twinkle in Blake's eye had extended to his mouth, which was grinning from ear to ear. There stood Durill squeezed in between two pillars.

" Yes, I want you, Miss May."

" What for, Durill ?"

" Nothing particular, only I like your company and assistance."

" And is that what you sent for me for?"

" Precisely, and also because I was not going to leave you to the tender mercies of Madam and Mrs. Calvert, who would pluck the peacock alive if she wanted his feathers, and fancied they would make her look prettier."

May did not reply to this speech, and when they reached the cosy snuggery Judy met them with—

" So you are not in bits, May ?"

"No, she is not, I took good care of her. But, 'pon my honour, Minnie has cheek enough for a dozen. She actually wanted May to go and see to her children while she disported her charming person at various parties. Of course Madam thought it perfectly correct. But I did not, so they had to content themselves with old nurse."

"I suspected it would be that; I am astonished at Minnie."

"That is more than I am. I know exactly what to expect from a yellow haired Drever now. They are thoroughly selfish and greedy."

"Let us be charitable, Durill."

"Very well, May darling, only don't forget my plan in the midst of so much charity."

"Self, self, Mr. Durill."

"No, May, not self, only care. I cannot afford to lose my labour; that would be 'wilful waste,' and we are told it is generally succeeded by 'woful want.'"

Durill Drever was educated for an engineer, and although he was not compelled to follow the business, he did so. He was extremely clever, and made a handsome sum each year; he was a kind hearted, sensible man. He was always ready to lend a helping hand in a good cause, but he could not tolerate indolence.

One evening, just after dinner, May was talking to the children by the fire before putting them into their beds. Parker had gone to her supper. May liked best to have them all to herself. She was sitting on a low chair, beside the old-fashioned nursery grate, holding little Evelyn in her arms warming her toes, and Ivo had a stool at her feet.

" Aunty May, do you hear the wind?"

" Yes, Ivo, it is high to-night."

" Evelyn is not afraid, Aunty May."

" No, I should think not. Evelyn is quite as safe in the wind as in the sunshine."

" Is Heaven a long way off, Aunty May?"

"No, Ivo, it is quite near, much nearer to some of us than we suspect. Why do you ask if it is a long way off?"

"Because I was thinking about it, and the 'Golden Ladder' Jacob dreamt of. I wonder when I shall run up that ladder, Aunty May?"

"When our Father wants you, Ivo."

"And sha'n't I go too, Aunty May."

"Yes, dear, I hope so."

"Wid you?"

"No, perhaps not with me, Evelyn, but I hope to come to you, if I do not go before."

"My toe tickles."

"Does it? then you are too near to the fire, Ivo."

"Then I will move. Look, Aunt May, here is Uncle Durill."

"Yes, Ivo, Uncle Durill is here; he has been standing in the doorway listening to you little people talking."

" Aunt May, are these children to be lifted into bed ?"

" Yes, please, Uncle Durill. They are nice and warm now."

Both were laid down and tucked in comfortably. The last kiss was repeated half a dozen times, till Durill declared there would be no end to the " last kiss."

" Aunty May," called a small voice when they had reached the door. " Aunty May."

" Yes, Evelyn ; what is it, love ?"

Evelyn had raised her sunny head off the pillow, and her eyes shone like stars in the fire light.

" Aunty May, paps I won't be here in the morning."

" Then where will you be, Evelyn ?"

" Done to Heaven, Aunty May."

" Well, that is not far away, and I shall know where you are."

" But you will cry, won't you, Aunty May ?"

"I don't know, darling. I should cry if you were lost, but you won't be lost there; I shall know where to find you. Now go to sleep, dear."

The child lay down quite happy and secure. Angels spread their wings over that little white bed, and Evelyn floated to dreamland.

Durill stopped when they were in the day nursery.

"May, I heard what you said to the children. I was listening. Do they always speak of heaven like that?"

"Yes, always. They did not know anything when they came; their mother or the nurse had taught them a short prayer, but they knew nothing about heaven or their Father."

"But they seemed to speak so happily and freely about it."

"Well, and why should they not? Is it not to be their home? I don't approve of always keeping children away, making them stand off in

a respectful, awed sort of way. I like to lead
them to talk about it—to make them acquainted
with God and heaven. Those little things don't
dread the idea of going up there—they like the
thought. They know nothing to fear in death.
It is not death to them. They fully expect to find
themselves up there some morning instead of in
the nursery. Heaven is to them a charming
place, where we shall all be together like here."

"But, May, do you believe that, like here?"

"Yes, certainly, Durill, why not? I believe
it will be a great deal nicer than here, but yet I
expect we shall all be together the same. What
do you imagine Ivo and Evelyn would do all by
themselves? If it is not going to be that way,
how do you think it is going to be?".

"May, I don't know; I never, to tell the truth,
thought about it. It was always represented to
my mind as too serious a subject to be weighed
and considered in a common way."

"Precisely. The little things are told to 'Hush,' and they sit like mice with long faces while the Scripture story is being told, which to them is perfectly uninteresting and unintelligible, for the reason that the characters are as highly coloured as possible; and they are much too solemn personages to be thought about like anyone else. There is not a more difficult task than to try and make a child understand anything it has not seen and cannot be shown. That was I believe why God sent his Son upon earth, that by daily seeing and hearing Him, the people might get interested and love Him. Now, I cannot see how a child is to love anyone it does not know, and the only way to make a child love God, is by constantly talking to it, and allowing it to talk of its Father—not in a serious, hushed manner, but confidently and cheerfully, making the little thing feel at home with Him. Letting it know that He is near to it, listening to what it

has got to say. What is so beautiful and rest-
ful as the thought that heaven is not far away,
and that we can reach our Father's hand by
stretching out ours? That the journey is so
short, almost like these two rooms, only a door
between, which will open when we knock. Durill,
those children are never afraid to go to bed in
the dark, because they know they are not *alone*.
I often hear them prattling away to each other
about heaven, and who they expect to have with
them. There is something wonderfully holy in a
child's trust. They never doubt anything I tell
them. They go to sleep each night with their
little heads running upon heaven, and I never
have any fears for them. They are not under
earthly protection."

" May, you are making me feel like the babies.
I wish I were one of them, to have you talk to
me so. But I must not forget what brought me

up after you.   Mark has come in, and he is asking for you."

"Oh, and you have let me wander off, and
Mark waiting all this time.   Where is he?"

"In the library, he would not go into the
drawing-room; he does not seem all right."

They hurried down and found Mark leaning
with his arms on the mantelpiece, and his head
bent, looking into the fire.   He turned at May's
entrance.

CHAPTER VI.

" How are you, Mark—anything the matter?"

" Yes, I think so, May."

He stooped to kiss her bright young face. They were brother and sister, and loved each other dearly.

Mark Calvert was a good-looking fellow; he had a kind sweet face, and his lightish brown hair was rather wavy.

" Mark, you are tired; sit here?"

May wheeled a comfortable chair to the fire.

" Have you had any dinner, Mark?"

" No, May, I have not; but I am not inclined for any?"

" Well, you must have some tea.   Durill and
I are very fond of playing truant from the drawing-room ; so we three will have some tea here."

Durill rang and gave the orders.

" What is to do, Mark, are the children
worse ?"

" No, May, it is not that ; they are getting
better, thank heaven.   But I feel weary and dis-
quieted ; I want someone to talk to me and
cheer me.   It is so lonely at home."

" Lonely, Mark !   Why, what has become of
Minnie ?"

" Oh ! she has gone to some party at the
Mortons.   At least she told me she intended
going when I saw her in about two."

" Have you not been home since two, Mark ?
Wherever have you been to ?"

" A long way, May.   But to tell you the
truth, I had no horse to-day, and that has made
me so tired and late."

" How is that?"

" Why, the new one fell lame, Durill, as you prognosticated, and Minnie wanted the brougham for this party, because she says the village flys are so dirty."

May felt very much ashamed of her sister. She, in her selfishness, would let her husband work himself to death, but she would go to the parties and take the only horse into the bargain.

" Why did you not send for a horse, Mark?"

" I really don't know, Durill; but if you could lend me one I should be obliged."

" You shall have a horse by all means. Shall I order a trap and take you home and send the horse in the morning, or will you ride it?"

" Thanks, I will ride it. But I am so busy, everyone is ill at once, and some such bad cases, and old Tinley has gone away for a week or two. I was called up three times last night. Minnie declares the people do it on purpose."

" Why do you not have an assistant, Mark ?"

" Well, I don't care about them, May; they are a great nuisance, and if anything goes wrong you are blamed. When I had Green half the people would not have him, so I found it was of no use. But I did think of asking Crispin to help me just for a day or two with the light cases, such as dressings."

" Yes, Crispin could help you, I am sure; it would teach him too. But can I do anything for you ?"

" Well, May, if you would call and see some of the poor things I should be glad; of course nothing infectious, but some of the old people. Minnie does not like it, and I don't care to press her. But you cannot imagine what a help it is. A woman finds out so much quicker than a man their wants; besides, I have no time to stay and talk to them. Then, if you would make a list out I would see it attended to. Tinley told me to get anything made or cooked at his house. That is another thing Minnie does not like, having soup and stuff made in the kitchen."

" How is the poor fellow who was crushed at Ashworth, Mark ?"

" Going on capitally, Durill. (A little more sugar, please, May.) The worst case on hand just now is Mother Parfait."

" What is to do with her ? She was walking in the village a few days since."

" Yes she was, poor old woman. But her son-in-law, Mason, died a day or two back, and the night before last she went to keep her daughter company after the funeral. I suppose they got some gin to soothe them in their grief, and the consequence was they fell asleep. Mother Parfait must have been too near to the candle, for the old creature succeeded in setting fire to her head. Her daughter was so muddled that it was some time before she could either put it out or get assistance, and the old woman is fearfully burnt. I don't expect her to recover."

"Oh, Mark, how dreadful! How she must suffer!"

"Not so much, May; that is one comfort. She has been unconscious nearly all the time since. But it would be a great blessing if God would take her, for she cannot possibly get over it. Her age is against her for one thing, even if the burns had not been so severe. I really think gin is woman's curse. I have more trouble through that spirit than anyone knows of."

"Yes, it is; I agree with you, Mark. But this is not an every-day occurrence, thank goodness, and perhaps it may be a warning to others."

"No; cases like Mother Parfait's are, comparatively speaking, few; but there is, according to my idea, even a more distressing case than hers not far from here."

"Who is it, Mark?"

"I don't think you know the person, Durill, or, in fact, any of the family. They have only just come. They live in that white house below the mill."

"Yes, I know the place."

"Their name is Trotter; they have been there about three months, may be not so much. One evening soon after they arrived I was sent for, and when I got there I found it was to attend Mrs. Trotter. She was in a high fever, and excessively irritable. I treated her accordingly; but the fever still held its ground, and I could not discover what ailed the old lady. I never had had such a puzzling case before. Mr. Trotter and the sons went to business each day, and I could never catch them. They are very well-to-do people. There is no daughter, but a niece of Mr. Trotter's—a Miss Whitcher. Perhaps you may have noticed her at church—a pretty girl, with light hair?"

" Yes, I fancy I have."

" Well, I resolved to see Miss Whitcher privately, and accordingly called one morning about ten, when I knew Mrs. Trotter would be in bed. I saw Miss Whitcher, and told her exactly my dilemma, and asked her to tell me if her aunt gave way? She confessed at once; poor girl, I felt for her. The woman drinks that cursed gin; does not take it to excess always, but systematically, and she is killing herself as fast as she can."

" And can nothing be done, Mark? Why not take it from her ?"

" Ah, there it is, May! Once let gin get hold of a woman, and you can never take it away ; they cannot do without it. Mr. Trotter did try and she was dying inch by inch. She has no appetite, and is never contented or happy, except when she is muddled. So that there is nothing for it, but to let her have it as long as she lives, which will not be long ; softening of the brain is going on rapidly, and she is killing herself slowly but surely."

" What must those sons think of their mother ?"

" Nothing at all, May ; they never trouble about her. When you cease to respect, you cease to love. I daresay they will be thankful when she is dead."

" What a shocking story. Let me give you another cup of tea, Mark."

" Half a cup, please, May. And how are your children ?"

" My children ! They are as much Durill's as mine. They are quite well, thank you ; I left them going to sleep."

" They are sweetly pretty, and greatly admired, May ; they have such nice manners. Lucy, I fear, is getting cross ; she seems to me peevish. I mentioned it to Minnie, but she had not noticed it. I have an idea that a mother should be a good deal with her children, and teach the little things; but my wife tells me that is a 'man's notion.'"

"You are perfectly correct, Mark; that is my notion, too. When Ivo and Evelyn came here, they were pretty tractable children, but they were nothing like what they are now, and I attribute it all to May's care and training."

"Nonsense, Durill! Mark, you must not heed him."

"But I do, May, and, what is more, believe it. I wish I could send you my little ones."

He sighed wearily. Was it possible that his eyes were getting opened to the faults and inability of his wife? Did he guess that she cared more for her own ease and comfort than the welfare of her children? Had she fallen short where a wife ought to be ever ready—in cheering and assisting her husband when things looked

dark; by her wise counsel strengthening him
and arming him again for the fight? Had he
found out that the greatest blessing a man can
have is not a lovely face? Let us pull a veil
down and shut out bitter truths. We will not
pick to pieces pretty Minnie Calvert. God made
her. Ah me! I wonder who or what is to
blame when a plant runs to seed?

"It is time I was off. Is Crispin about,
May? because I should like to see him."

"Oh! yes, Crispin is in. But won't you
come to the drawing-room, Mark? they are all
there, and papa would like to see you."

"Not this evening, I think, May; though I
am very much refreshed, and all the better for
seeing your face. Lois is in the drawing-room,
of course?"

"Yes; don't you hear the piano? She is
enchanting Archer with sweet melody."

"Durill, don't sneer," laughed May.

The handsome mouth was sarcastically twisted, and a wicked glitter in the large brown eyes.

" Well, May, I did not intend to sneer ; but really Lois' music is one of the things I cannot understand or appreciate. She sits gracefully enough, never by any chance crushing the arrangement of balloons at the back, and manages to turn up her eyes and sigh divinely just at the proper moment. But I can't admire the sounds nor yet the art. Bad taste, I suppose. Archer seems to like it, for I left him hanging over the chair and looking unutterable things at the sweet creature."

" Now, Durill, Lois is considered a great beauty, only brothers are most ungrateful things. They never can admire their own sisters. But I will go and find Crispin for you, Mark."

May went and found Crispin lolling, talking to Madam, while Lois was making eyes at Archer, and warbling " We may be happy yet."

Good looking Edward Archer was deeply in love it was plainly to be seen; he was on the brink of desperation; he only wanted a little push to send him toppling over, and when he came to his senses again he would find Miss Lois blushing, and murmuring something purposely incoherent about " papa." No doubt " We may be happy yet" was intended as a *coup de grace,* for she was an adept at flirting, and knew exactly the state of her victim, how far he had gone in the " *grande passion*," and how many beats his heart was making to the minute. But the unexpected entrance of May broke the spell, and Mr. Archer turned to her politely and moved a chair.

" I am not staying, Mr. Archer; don't disturb yourself, I only want Crispin."

Lois shot an angry glance at May: well, it was unfortunate.

" Want me, May? What is it?"

Crispin shook back his curls and raised his

pretty face. There was something visionary in the sweet beauty of those yellow-haired Drevers. They seemed never to cease being children; always wanting to be petted and caressed. Crispin was a man well grown, yet his face expressed weakness of intellect and indecision. His doting mother had evidently been playing with those golden curls. He had no moustache or whiskers, and there was no show of them, even sideways. His chin was beautifully white and delicate; his mouth was curved like a girl's, and his eyes were cold, glittering, and hard, like polished steel. Nature had forgotten nothing to make Crispin Benton Drever beautiful. I cannot call that style of beauty in a man handsome, but an attentive observer would have found out that there was something short. It did not exist in face, form, or features, it was this—Crispin Drever had no soul. He was heartless. It was no use appealing to his feelings or sympathy, he did not possess either. Tell him a touching story, chain his attention for a few seconds, and congratulate yourself that you had him. The next moment he would wriggle through your hands with glittering eyes, laughing and showing his pretty teeth, and stroll away blowing you a kiss on the tips of his taper fingers as he went. Madam called it " a charming flow of spirits ; but the Bentons were always so irresistible."

" Yes, I want you, Crispin, or rather Mark does. Will you come ?"

" When did Mark come, May ?"

" A little time since, mamma; he has been a long round, and he wants to speak to Crispin."

May put in the " long round " as a sort of excuse. Madam was a great one for politeness, and no doubt she considered that Mark ought to have come and paid his court to her.

" Do you know what it is Mark wants me for, May ?"

" Of course she does," chimed in Lois, who had come, like all the rest of busy people, to hear the news. " May is the receptacle for secrets, especially those belonging to Durill, Mark, Julius, and half a dozen more. Don't you perceive how extremely wise she looks ?"

" Ah ! that accounts for you giving us so little of your society, Miss May ?"

" How so, Mr. Archer ? I think I see a great deal of you all, only sometimes I am occupied."

" Yes, Mr. Archer," replied the Squire, " we should all fare badly without May; she is of great assistance to me."

" Crispin, are you coming ?" again asked May ; she feared to leave him, for then, perhaps, he might not come at all. He liked the lounge and pillows.

" Yes, Miss Determination ; lead the way."

In the middle of the wide hall Crispin called out—

" I say, May, stop a minute.   What is it Mark wants, because I hate being bored?"

May smiled.

" I know that quite well by this time.   But I don't think you will dislike it, or call it a bore."

" I don't know what May has brought me for, Mark," said Crispin, as they shook hands, " perhaps you will kindly explain.   May is worse than one of the ' Secret Brethren,' nothing can be screwed out of her."

" And a great blessing, too, Crispin; nothing is worse than a babbling woman.   But this is no secret, only I suppose May prudently adopts the same rule for everything strictly not her own property.   The fact is, I want your help for a few hours each day.   I am dreadfully busy, and if you would do a little for me in the mornings I should take it as a great kindness.   Tinley has gone away for a few weeks, and I am quite thrown, what with his patients and my own.   The clubs take up so much time, and the poor things must be attended to."

" Why don't they have a doctor entirely for the clubs, Mark ?"

" Because the poor fellows could never live, May. The pay is wretched, and half you don't get. Well, there are not sufficient of the better class to support three of us, so there it is. It would be all right if Tinley were at home."

" Yes, Mark, I will help with pleasure if the people will let me."

" Oh, yes ; I will give you nothing dangerous or responsible, but the indoor patients are the worst. My surgery was chock full this morning, and I could not make all the medicines up in time. as it was."

" All right ; 1 will be down in the morning."

" Won't you come into the drawing-room, Mark ?"

" No, not to-night, Crispin. I must be off

home; it is getting close upon nine, I see, so good night."

"Good night; my love to Minnie, and tell her I shall be down to see her soon."

Crispin lounged away to the drawing-room, and Mark indulged in a smile.

Mark Calvert had a wonderful smile, it was like a sunbeam. It quivered and danced over his face for long, and the light was a long while dying out. May liked to get him to smile for that reason. It was such a rare beauty, and little Arnold had it; his baby face would light up in just the same way when anything pleased him. Lucy was not so, she was like her mother.

CHAPTER VII.

" WHAT has amused you, Mark ?"

"Nothing much, Durill, only Crispin's face.
I never expected him to yield with so good a
grace. But I rather fancy he will be obliged
to turn up his sleeves yet, unless the Squire
means to buy him a swell practice at the West
End."

" Ah, that won't be in your time or mine,
Mark. The Squire is one of the old school; he
believes in young men showing themselves worth
something before they get promoted. And he
will not do what Crispin wishes I know. He
will give him a fair start, and the rest he must

do for himself. But if he does no better than Gilbert why the start will be money wasted."

" Yes, by Jove! Gilbert has made a nice mess of it. I cannot think what he has been after."

" I can though ; he is just like the rest of the yellow-haired ones, made to lie in soft places. If poverty came to you, Mark, old fellow, you would prove to your cost the truth of my words."

" God forbid I ever should, Durill; that would be a bitter day to me. Yet I know perfectly well what you say is true. But, God helping me, I will never put her to the test."

Mark spoke solemnly, reverently. He would fight the good fight to the last, and when did God ever forget to reward any of his soldiers? Ah, Minnie Calvert, you had drawn a prize out of the lottery, where so many draw blanks !

" Hush ! There's the court-yard clock calling nine. I ought to have been home by now; but I

don't often indulge. Good night, May, love.
Come, Durill, is that horse ready?"

"Yes; I will go with you. May, don't go
away—I mean to bed; if you do, leave your
dressing-room door open, so that I may come in
when I return."

"Oh, I am not a go-to-bed-early, but I may
be up-stairs. I always keep a good fire up there.
Mark, you would laugh to see some of the sights
in my dressing-room. They all come flocking in
with something to say, and there's quite a meet-
ing. I dare not lock the door, else they would
go on tapping away for half-an-hour."

"By the way, it's your room, is it not, where
there's 'hot coffee' from half-past eleven till
one?"

May and Durill burst out laughing.

"May, I think it is time we did start the
coffee business again, it was awfully jolly!"

"Yes, I wanted some last night myself. So

you have heard of that, Mark? Well, it was Julius who commenced it. He has it in his chambers, and he asked me about it, so I got everything arranged, kettle and all, and I used to make this said coffee every night. It was so nice; we three had it all to ourselves for some time, and then the others found us out, and would come too. Lois declared she smelt it. After that I had to get more cups, and there they used to come, one after the other, and it was really capital fun. We kept it up all winter. But one morning there were some lines pasted on my door; something about a ' wayside inn, kept by Dame May, who supplied excellent hot coffee from eleven to one.' Julius wrote them, and it caused such a laugh. Yes, Durill, I really think I must tell Ellen to bring up the things again."

"Do, by all means; to-night if you choose, my dear."

They both went off to the stables, leaving May alone, so she suddenly bethought herself that she had not been into the drawing-room all the evening, and Madam was straight-laced on some subjects. So she bent her steps that way. May was not a beauty, but still she was far from ugly. Her face was rather brown, with a dash of paleness through it. Her eyes were splendid, full, large brown eyes. They were not those languishing eyes that are thought so much about. They lacked that dreamy expression, except at times. But always they were clear and intelligent, with a calm, steady light burning in them.

May was wonderfully calm, from a child she had been so, and now as a woman it was more noticeable. It amounted almost to fascination. She was always neat, but never showily dressed, and there was that repose of manner which alone springs from a clear, unruffled conscience. She was strong in mind, yet tender-hearted; her gentle firmness was a special gift of God's, and her common sense rendered her an able adviser. To-night she wore a plain dress of black silk, getting rather shabby, too, but it did not look amiss on stately May. She entered the drawing-room quietly, and did not want to attract attention. She enjoyed sitting in a corner and looking on. There was one window that May always sat in, if possible; it was in one angle of the large room, and quite an observatory; it commanded, by its peculiar position, a full view of the entire room.

This evening, however, she could not reach it because the Squire called her, and she had to content herself with a seat in the midst of the chattering people. Lois was radiant in a new dress, and flirting away with Ted Archer; but she had taken good care to station herself out of sight of the Squire.

"May, has Mark gone?"

" Yes, papa, and I think Durill has gone with him; to the stables, at least, to see about a horse."

" What about a horse? Anything to do with Mark's?"

" Yes; one is sick, so Durill is going to lend him one."

" Quite right; but Durill is always kind and thoughtful."

This was said for only May and himself to hear; but the first part Crispin had caught, and he turned sharply and called—

" May, I want you for a second."

" What is it, Crispin?" asked May, glancing into his flushed face.

" Why has Durill gone to the stables?"

" To get a horse for Mark; did you not hear me tell papa?"

" Yes, but I did not clearly understand; he does not usually visit the stables so late."

" Well, but there is a reason to-night."

" What reason ?" asked Crispin, crossly. " I wish you would speak out, May, and tell me the truth. What has taken Durill to the stables ?"

This conversation was spoken rather low, and they were not very close to the rest. May's eyes flashed slightly, but she was quite calm, as usual.

" Crispin, you are sadly out of temper, and not too polite to me. I have told you the reason twice over, and I am not in the habit of speaking anything but the truth."

She gently moved away to her favourite window, and Crispin went to be petted by his mother.

When Durill and Mark reached the court-yard, there were several men going about with lanterns and buckets, which at nine at night was unusual, especially when there was no one going out, and Madam had not had the carriage that day. In fact, the entire place was alive, and the principal scene of the commotion was a stable at the far end. A lantern stood in the window, and the door wide open, while several grooms with their caps on one side and their hands on their hips were bunting their heads together, as first one and then another laid down the law, and stated his experience. One suggested a pint of whisky, another one of hot ale, but high above the rest rose the voice of Jenkinson, the fat old coachman. He rarely drove now, but he was head of the department, and appealed to on all occasions.

" I fear this will prove an uncommon bad business, she looks so blowed. Bob, just you get on the grey cob and go over for Patterson, and bring him back with you ; and someone else step over and ask Blake to send Mr. Durill here. Won't he be wild though ! my stars ! but best let him know at once. Be quick, whoever's going

for him. Miss May, too, how put out she'll be!
Law's sake! I would sooner had it any on 'em
than hers. Poor Gipsy! poor lass—poor lass!"

At this stage in the performance Durill and
Mark entered.

" Why, Jenkinson, what is to do here?"

" Eh! Mr. Durill, glad to see you, sir. I was
just sending for you. We're in a mess, sir.
This 'ere Gipsy of Miss May's is taken bad, and
it is so sudden like; she was all right at half-past
five, for I was in."

" I am afraid it is serious, Jenkinson; have
you sent for Patterson?"

" Yes, sir, Bob has gone; I sent him just
as you came in."

" Mark, what do you think about her," asked
Durill, stroking the poor beast.

It stood with head hanging down, starting
eyes, and expanded nostrils, while its sides were
going like a pair of bellows. Its breathing was

loud, and evidently the animal was in great pain. Mark's answer was a prolonged whistle, and he looked at Gipsy long and carefully.

" I should say this mare has been over ridden, Jenkinson."

" Over ridden, Mr. Calvert !" exclaimed plump Jenkinson, catching his breath almost as badly as the mare in his astonishment. " Why, bless you, sir, Gipsy has never been out since Miss May rode her along with Mr. Durill here, except for exercise in the Paddock with one of the boys, and me looking on all the while. No, sir, it's not *that*, I'll take my 'davy, though it is just like it. And that is what is puzzling me so, 'cause I never saw it except in cases of over riding."

" Well, Jenkinson, it really seems more like that to me than anything else ; but since you assure me the mare has not been out, why I must give way to you."

" I agree with Mr. Calvert, Jenkinson. This

mare has been shamefully pushed; I should not be surprised if she dies before morning. It is that and nothing else that ails her."

" Law's sakes, Mr. Durill, sir, how positive you are; believe me, sir, the mare has not been out."

Old Jenkinson looked extremely hurt at being doubted by Durill, whom he had taught to ride, and taken his first day out with the hounds.

" Well, well, Jenkinson, I am not doubting you, but I still believe this mare has been out. Do you think it possible anyone could take her without your knowledge?"

Most of the men had slunk off when Durill and Mark entered the stable, but when Durill asked Jenkinson that question the two who were there went out. It was a curious question to put, and the men felt rather delicate about it, no doubt.

Jenkinson assumed his gravest manner and considered profoundly for a second.

"No, Mr. Durill, I think that would be quite impossible, because my cottage is at the bottom of the court yard, and I always sits close at the window, so that if anyone had passed while I was at my tea I should have seen them go through the gates. But I am inclined to your way of thinking, sir. This mare puts me just in mind of the Squire's Prince, as that London gentleman killed that run with the Slapston Hounds. You mind that, Mr. Durill?"

"Yes, very well, Jenkinson. Poor Prince! The Squire was awfully cut up about that. The man was a complete fool; he rode like a madman. Prince was a splendid animal, but the fellow had no sense. He did for him, any how."

"Aye, that he did. Well, this mare do put me in mind of Prince, I must say; but I cannot imagine how it has come about."

Jenkinson scratched his bald head in his perplexity. It was enough to puzzle the old man, because he knew perfectly well it had not gone out with his permission, neither had he seen it go.

" I have kept order here these thirty years, Mr. Durill, and never had such a thing to happen before to me. I can't believe as any one of the boys would dare to take it out without my orders : why, they are all good lads, every one on 'em."

" I believe that, yet I cannot otherwise account for the poor thing's condition. I hope Patterson will not be long coming. However, we can do no good standing here, and you want to get home, Mark.

" Jenkinson, have the brown mare that used to draw Madam's brougham saddled for Mr. Calvert. She will carry you nicely, Mark, and go in your brougham too."

" Thanks, that will do capitally. Durill, I could take my oath this mare has been hardly ridden."

They had both gone close up to the poor panting creature ; it was now lying on its side.

" Yes, I am certain we are correct, and I shall have it sharply seen to, I can promise you. May will be awfully grieved."

" Your horse is ready, Mr. Calvert, " said Jenkinson, appearing at the door."

" All right. Jenkinson, look here, I wish you to enquire from the grooms who has had this mare out, and if Patterson comes before long send for me, I want to see him."

" Certainly, Mr. Durill ; but I am very much afraid it is a bad case ; she can't stand now."

Durill saw Mark ride off, and then crossed over the court yard and into the gardens. He walked up and down the gravel walk, puffing away at his cigar. He was angry, and striding about in the moonlight, he looked a very undesirable foe for anyone to possess. He seemed to forget his dress-boots, but then the ground was frosty. Presently his quick ear caught the sound of horse's hoofs in the court-yard, so he walked back and met Patterson as he was getting out of his gig.

Together they went to the stable, and Patterson looked at the animal in rather an astonished manner, and then at those gathered round.

"What is to do with the mare, Patterson?"

"The mare has been over-ridden, Mr. Drever. She won't live half-an-hour; I can do nothing. What on earth have you been about, Jenkinson?"

"Me? Nothing! I am just at my wits' end; the mare has never been out of the stable. I can swear she was all right at half-past five, for I was in here myself; and when I came again at a quarter to nine she was blowing, and since then she has got worse."

"There is something decidedly wrong here, Jenkinson, and I will have it investigated at once.   Call the men.   It is your opinion that the mare is dying from over-riding, Patterson ?"

"Most certainly, Mr. Drever."

The men had not left, those who lived near or on the premises, which most did, and they all entered the stable looking extremely sheepish. Durill spoke to them shortly and strangely.

"Mr. Patterson states this mare to be dying from over-riding, and I want the man who rode it to come forward and say so, or if anyone knows about it let him come forward.   I shall assuredly find it out, so by telling now it will save a great deal of trouble."

There was a deep silence for a moment, and then a man pushed his way to the front.   He was a nice looking young fellow, very thin. He twisted his cap about, and looked at Durill in some fear.

"If you please, sir, I know who had Gipsy out."

" Who was it ?—speak, man."

" Mr. Crispin, sir."

" Mr. Crispin !—are you sure, Cummings ?"

"Yes, quite, Mr. Jenkinson. He came into the yard soon after the clock had gone seven, and I met him, he told me to get this mare saddled quickly. I did so, and him standing here watching me. I did not know I was doing wrong, as it was for one of the gentlemen, sir."

"And Mr. Crispin went out on it?" asked Durill.

"Yes, sir."

" But I will take my solemn oath he did not go through the court-yard gate," almost shouted Jenkinson, in his excitement.

" No, he did not go out that way, sir, he went through the paddock and down the cart road."

" And what time did he return ?" asked Durill.

" About eight, sir, and I took the mare from

him in the paddock. He made me wait there till he came back."

" And why did you not tell of this sooner, when you heard me making enquiries ?"

The man looked terribly confused, and while twirling his cap round, jerked out—

" Mr. Crispin told me not to tell, sir."

" That will do my man, you may all go."

CHAPTER VIII.

It was no use questioning any further. That Crispin had killed the poor thing there was not the slightest doubt, but for what purpose had he taken such a ride, and where had he gone to? Durill's handsome face was quite pale, as he turned to old Jenkinson—

"Don't say any more about it, Jenkinson. No doubt Mr. Crispin can explain it, and it won't do to fill everyone's mouth."

"I understand, Mr. Durill; I understand. But law's sakes, what can have made Master Cris ride like that? Mr. Crispin, I should say, but it seems only yesterday he was Master Cris."

No one answered Jenkinson's question. Durill was not able to, and it was no business of Patterson's. Gipsy was dying fast, and it was a hard death, poor beast. How she laboured and struggled for breath, her intelligent eyes almost out with agony, as she fought with her grim foe death. A few more moments, and Gipsy was still; so Patterson left, and drove home to the bosom of his family. Durill wished old Jenkinson good-night, and walked to the house. It was now twenty minutes past ten, and the piano was still going. This time May was the performer, by desire of the Squire, who was just napping a little.

Durill was in a towering rage, and his great square shoulders looked broader than ever, as, catching sight of Blake with the glasses, he called out—

"Here, Blake, take my coat!"

The old man came with an anxious expression

on his face, and after taking a good look at the stern face above him, he said—

"No offence, Mr. Durill, but it might frighten the Squire if you was sharp with Mr. Crispin in his presence, and he has not yet gone to bed, sir."

Durill glanced at the old man, and a smile rose to his lips.

"Don't be afraid, Blake, I am not going to chastise Mr. Crispin, though I feel quite equal to it; but perhaps I had better not annoy my father by making a row."

Blake did well to speak, since Durill's feelings agreed with his appearance. God help Crispin if he had chastised him.

The news of the mare's death had reached the servants' hall, and Blake ventured to remark how Miss May would fret.

"Yes, poor girl, she is always getting put upon, and she liked Gipsy so, she carried her beautifully. Just ask Miss May to come to me when you go in, Blake."

"Yes, sir."

Blake seemed quite relieved that Durill was not going into the drawing-room.

In a few moments May appeared.

"What a time you have been, Durill. Did you go home with Mark?"

"No, love, I did not, but I have been kept in the stables. May, something has happened to Gipsy, but I will buy you another, dear."

"Oh! Durill, is Gipsy dead?"

"Yes, May, she is, and I am awfully distressed about it, because the poor creature did not die fairly."

May's large eyes were full of tears.

"I liked Gipsy so much—she was so gentle— and also because you gave her to me. But what do you mean by did not die fairly, Durill?"

" Why, —— it, I can't help it, May, I am just wild. She was ridden to death."

" By whom ?"

" That young scamp, Crispin. He may thank his stars I did not meet him just now, but for Blake I should have given him a jolly good thrashing. But it is better as it is, the Squire might have been put out."

"Yes, Durill, I am glad it did not come to that, it would have quite upset papa and mamma, and made such a talk. But where did he go to, and why take my poor Gipsy ?"

" I don't know, May. I shall certainly speak to Crispin in the morning, but I promise to keep my temper. There is something very queer about it. He sneaked off after dinner by the cart road, and bribed one of the men, Cummings, or some such name, not to tell. He came back about eight, in time for tea, you see; the groom put the mare up, and never said a word to any one.

When Jenkinson went his nightly round, a little before nine, she was blowing awfully, and when Mark and I went over at nine the place was up. Jenkinson was certain the mare had never been out, and no one could make anything of it. But when Patterson came he at once pronounced the mare to be dying, and from the effects of over riding. I had the men called, and this Cummings confessed. Gipsy died just before I left the stable. But, May, darling, don't grieve; I will go to town to-morrow and buy you another."

May looked at Durill quietly.

" Thank you, Durill, I will not have another."

" May!"

" No, I will never have another; I liked Gipsy, and she has gone; I will not have another to go."

Her face was perfectly pale, and her pretty white hands (one of her few charms) were clasped tightly.

" But, May love, I want you to go out with me ; surely you won't refuse to do that ?"

" No, Durill, indeed I won't; but I can ride anything that is steady. Jenkinson can find me some old animal, I dare say, and it will do quite nicely."

Durill was quite troubled.

" I would sooner anything had happened than this. I knew how it would be with you. But can't you put your affections on another? I will get it as like Gipsy as possible."

"No, I can't. I shall like Gipsy just the same when they have put her in a hole in some field. I gave her all the love I could give to a horse, and I cannot take it back. Never mind, brother; don't say any more about it."

Durill looked at her in astonishment, but she had been so from a child. She could not transfer her affections. He took her in his arms; he knew her worth.

" Little May, you are too true hearted; if all women were like you it would be a bad look out, one half would be widows and the other half disappointed maidens; and what do you suppose would become of a poor fellow like me?"

May laughed.

" You stupid thing, there are plenty of girls that would have you whether they had been disappointed or not. But I can't spare you just now, Durill, though I should like to see you happily married."

They sat and talked till the others were going up stairs, and reminded them that they ought to go to.

" There is no coffee to-night, I suppose, May?"

" No; I am sorry there is not. I quite forgot to tell Ellen, but you shall have it to-morrow night. By-the-bye, that reminds me; when will the instigator of that practice be here?"

" Julius ? Oh, the end of this month. No, what am I talking about? That would be to-morrow week—somewhere about the 17th of December, I fancy he wrote me."

At breakfast next morning Durill said to Crispin, " I want to say a word to you when you have finished."

Crispin glanced up, a smile on his face, and then devoted himself to a pie that was opposite. Anyone would have supposed that he had not the remotest notion of the nature of the business, he seemed so happy and unconcerned.

When they rose from the table Durill caught May by the arm and drew her out of the room with him, calling upon Crispin to follow. Crispin lounged after them in a few moments, and swinging himself on to the table, sat warming himself before the snuggery fire.

" Now then, Durill, be quick, because I promised to help Mark, and the patients come at ten."

It was quite evident that Durill had brought May to help him keep the devil down, for there was a lurid light in his eyes, as he leaned against the chimneypiece, with his strong arm round May.

"What made you take May's pad out, last night, Crispin ?"

" Oh, I wanted it, that was all."

This was said in a most indifferent off-hand tone, and May felt the arm round her tighten like a band of iron.

"That is no answer. I want to know why you took that any more than any of the others?"

" Well, I knew May had not been out on it lately, and I thought it might be the better for a little exerci se."

" Crispin, don't tell lies; your reason for taking Gipsy was because you imagined it would not be found out; it was a right down underhand trick, and I should like to know where you went to ? "

" That's my business."

" Come, young man, I'll just trouble you to be civil, it is the least you can do after killing the mare !"

" Killing the mare ? Who killed it ? I did not !"

" Yes, you did ; Gipsy died last night, in my presence, from being overridden. And the man Cummings confessed it was you. You ought to be ashamed of yourself, sir, to ride any animal like that. You can have been after no good, that is very certain. But I don't care to pry into your affairs, or I could easily track you. You sneaked off in the dark the cart way, and bribed the groom not to tell; it does not look too creditable, I must say, Crispin, independently of having ridden the poor brute to death, and deprived your sister of her horse. "

" She will get another, I have no doubt."

" No," thundered Durill, "she will not get

another, because she will not have one ; but you will get thrashed within an inch of your life, sir, if ever I catch you at the like game. If I had met you last night you would have had reason to repent it. Now, get out of my sight, quickly, else I may forget my good resolution."

Crispin saw that in big Durill's eye that warned him to be off ; besides he knew what a poor chance he had with his womanly hands against the man of iron. So muttering something about injustice, and telling the Squire, he escaped from the room.

Durill paced up and down like a caged lion, but presently he stopped before May, who stood calmly waiting, till he should be cooled. A softer light came into his eyes, and he smiled his old genial smile.

" Do you think me a brute, May ?"

" No, Durill, you know I don't, and you did keep your temper."

" Yes, after a fashion, but he exasperated me so, May; but for you, with that calm face of yours, I should have administered a few taps of correction. There is some devilment in it, I feel convinced."

" Yes, I did not like his manner over it, it was so dogged. But, Durill, to please me, let the matter drop. I am the loser, and I will abide by my loss, only don't let there be any disturbance about it. I think it better not to probe, we might find something we did not like."

" Why, May, you amaze me; this is something new, you used not to approve of bottling things up !"

" Nor do I now, but this case is not a common one; and besides we have to deal with one of our own—it makes a wonderful difference, Durill."

" But, come now, do you think it right to smother a fire? Don't you think it ought to be effectually put out? I do. If I had my way in this business I would set to work and discover what prompted Crispin to take that mysterious ride last night. Who knows but what we might prevent some pending evil ?"

" Very true, but here is another side to the question. Do you imagine that Crispin will have planned so badly that the motive will be near the top and ready for you to unearth without assistance ? No. Then by getting that assistance and ferreting you will fill other people's mouths, and make them regard Crispin with suspicion. Durill, there is nothing so difficult to deal with as cunning ; and at that Crispin is a match for anyone."

" Yes, I know he is ; but that I would rather try than wait. I dread anything when I cannot see it ; nothing is worse than an imaginary danger."

" Ah ! then upon that principle I suppose you got into bed backwards way when you were a juvenile, in case anyone might catch hold of you. But I understand what you mean and I share your feelings; and at the same time console myself with the thought that Crispin is so fond of himself and so cunning that he will plot and scheme and throw dust in people's eyes while he lives. He will manage somehow to make things appear smooth for himself, and those who want to find anything out about Crispin will have to dig a long way down."

"But how about chance, May? You know there is an old saying, ' Murder will out.' "

"Yes. Well, one cannot contend with chance. But I feel perfectly certain of one thing, whatever was Crispin's errand last night, bad, good, or indifferent, it will be hard work to bring it home to him. And as for his college doings and private scrapes, I don't believe his bosom friend Ted Archer knows anything about them, or if he does, Crispin has the whip hand of him, and he will never tell. Depend upon it Cris will find a way to stitch peoples' mouths up if they know anything to tell. Therefore I feel pretty safe."

" Well done, May; that is a grand argument, and since you understand him so well I shall trust to you keeping your 'weather eye open,' and singing out when it is getting hot."

" Yes, I intend to watch, no harm can come of that, and when the time comes, I will stave off the disgrace if possible, should there be any, for the sake of papa; but it is no use looking for it."

" In the meantime you will go on quietly and regularly with your duties, prudent May! We are also told to ' work while we can,' and ' improve each shining hour.' That reminds me, when are we to finish our talk?'

" What talk?"

" Why, the one Mark interrupted—our talk about heaven."

" Oh! any time you choose; all times are good to talk about that."

" Then let it be the very first time we are alone. It is useless trying over the coffee, because they all come in. I wonder whether Crispin will absent himself after this ?"

" I hope not; we won't allude to it again, for it is past and gone."

" Very well, May; better let it die away."

CHAPTER IX.

GIBBONS GROVE lay to the left of Wild Wood, in a clump of trees, and the Downs at its back. It was something like a Chinese house, and when the sun was on it looked as if of gold. It was ornamented with wood work and a verandah; a large field, on which grazed a goodly collection of North American bulls, separated it from the road.

The late William Calvert had been an attorney, much respected and beloved. He was a good husband and a good father. So when he was called away it was a sore parting. He left a wife and three children—Mark, comfortably settled as a doctor in the village, and to whom you have already been introduced, and two daughters, Kate and Ruby.

The hour is six, and being the end of November of course quite dark. The scene is the drawing-room of Gibbons Grove. After the death of Mr. Calvert there had been some retrenching, such as fewer servants, horses, carriages, &c., yet there was every comfort possible.

The house was not expensively furnished, and the things were getting the worse for wear, but by the light of the fire they looked extremely well. Especially, as sitting in a low chair at one side of the grate, was a pretty little thing curled up like a kitten, and just as soft and warm. A winsome little woman, with a pretty round figure, two great, loving, blue eyes, which, by reason of their long lashes, appeared violet, and a nose, which no one, however charitably disposed, could convert into anything more or less than a pug.

This little face was rather pale, not in consequence of being delicate, but simply because she took after her father, who possessed that ashy complexion.

Ruby Calvert was the same age as May Drever, and they were great friends; they had both gone to the same school, and learned to love each other for pure worth. Ruby was a sensible, tender-hearted little creature, though not so clear in intellect and determined as May, who was a shade taller, and in every way better able to battle with the world. So Ruby sat comfortably before the bright fire, silent, and with her soul full of happiness.

The room was not still, for it was filled with delicious melody.

Kate, Ruby's sister, was playing, and she could play—play the soul to sleep, and fill the heart with tender, loving thoughts. She was a wonderful clever girl, small, like Ruby, but not so plump. Considered by most people prettier, for, in place of the pale cheeks, she had two rosy ones, which irresistibly reminded one of two tempting apples. She was a blue-stocking, with all the charms and with none of the faults. She was not untidy or lazy. She was not always dabbling in ink and going about with holes in her stockings. She could make the puddings, keep the house, laugh, play, sing, draw, speak French irreproachably, feel for others, and go to sleep with an easy conscience, with her rosy little face peeping from between the pillows. She had a most intelligent face, and it was helped out by the eyeglass she was compelled to use, being slightly short-sighted, and which earned for her the name of " Professor."

Her music was decidedly of the superior kind; it was brilliant, and would bear scrutinizing; it was faultless. The touch was firm, without being heavy, and each note was clear and distinct. Combined with this was excellent execution and natural talent. One minute she could make you almost dance, and the next hush you to a serious turn of mind, softening down each trial and care, and carrying you away with the exquisite music.

This evening she was playing " Les Arpages" beautifully, and the firelight flickering up caught Ruby's face and showed that Kate had indeed played her soul away. Deep, deep down in the heart of the burning coals she saw a picture—it was sweet to her eyes. Suppose we look?

There, in the centre of that red clump, we see a road—a nice long, hard road, with woods here and there—on the frosty air is borne the faint tinkling of some far-off sheep-bell, while on that ivy-covered stump sits a robin singing a melancholy little song, the burthen of which would seem to be " A crumb, please, a crumb!" Coming along briskly, is a big man, wrapped in a brown top-coat, some papers in his hand, and a huge cigar in his mouth.

It is a great, big, towering figure, and appears above the hedges, but the handsome, kindly face does not scare the robin. Had that robin been a beggar, he would have received half-a-crown, in case there might be any little people at home with empty stomachs and blue limbs.

It is Durill Drever who has been to town, and is walking from the station. Strange to relate, Ruby Calvert has been walking, and they meet, and exchange greetings. And this is the little scene, only a few hours' old, that appears again to Ruby's eye in the redhot coal.

Ah, pretty Ruby ! " Love's young dream !" we have caught you at it, and it seems fitting, what with twilight, music, a glowing fire, and the great secret of all—nothing to do. Dream on about the big man, who has turned your little brain, and may that dream last long—may there be no bitter waking ; you have staked your all, poor child, in the great game of life. May angels waft their wings, and turn the wheel !

Presently the music ceased, and the fairies, blowing soft kisses to Ruby, vanished at the sound of Kate's cheery voice. She was as merry as a cricket when nothing serious was on hand.

"Dear me ! what time is it, Ruby ? Are you asleep ?"

"No, I am not."

"Well, next door to it, having only just awoke. But I do so want some tea."

Ruby rose and stretched her short neck to see the clock, whose golden hands showed the time to be ten minutes past six, of which fact Kate was duly apprised.

"Then tea must be ready, and I suppose mamma is making it instead of calling one of us."

" I wonder if Mark will come in to-night?"

" No, I don't suppose so; he is so busy just now, with Dr. Tinley being absent."

" Kate, what a queer thing it is we have not seen George Hardwick since he came down. Captain Hardwick said he would be coming. I really think it is extremely rude of him, don't you?"

Kate was busy poking the fire, and did not pay any attention to Ruby's remark, and the entrance of Mrs. Calvert prevented it being repeated.

Mrs. Calvert was rather short and stout, and decidedly fidgetty and nervous. Her health was but poor, and she at times imagined herself one of the most injured mortals on the face of the earth.

Many people considered her a sweet tempered woman, and she frequently took occasion to tell her children how she was noted for amiability in her youth. But, alas, they did not know her in

her youth, for Kate, Ruby, and Mark, were the
end of a large family, the boys all came first and
the girls last, and between Kate and Ruby there
was a difference of three and a half years. Now,
in the decline of life, Mrs. Calvert's amiability
only visited her by fits and starts, and her daughters required some little patience to deal with
her. They were both good girls ; they would
take care and stand by their mother to the last,
but perpetual fault-finding, discontent, helpless-
ness, and censuring, had shown them their
mother's true character, and rubbed off a good
deal of the freshness of affection. They knew
exactly where the quicksands lay, and their life
was one continual endeavour to walk round them.
Mrs. Calvert was ridiculously sensitive, always
suspicious, and feeling hurt about nothing. Then
would follow a violent fit of weeping, and a fair
sprinkling of temper as she bemoaned the loss of
her husband, and the unfeeling conduct and

cruelty of her children. After these periodical storms there came a lull, in which she would maintain the most tragic dignity, assert her authority, and pull the reins of government so tightly as almost to render the lives of Kate and Ruby wretched. She intended to do this, that, and the other, and would have no interference from anyone. "Remember I'm your mother," as if they were ever likely to forget. She had no idea on two or three occasions how near she was to being daughterless—how the bit had been chucked a little too rudely, and cut their mouths (which, by the way, were getting very hard). But they were not the kind of girls to sneak off with one of those wonderful little bundles which appear to contain everything, for one never by any chance hears of those much afflicted and beautiful young ladies having any washing done.

There was a great deal to arrange before they could leave their home and work for themselves, and during that period there was time for reflection.

Their father was dead; if they left their mother what would become of her? She would be left to the care of strangers. She would have no one to find fault with or worry, and that seemed to be the very prop of her existence. I wonder what a cow would do if it were deprived of its cud? Pine away perhaps. At any rate, it was intended to have it, so with Mrs. Calvert, and it might be dangerous to take it away, after she had chewed it so many years. And besides, they recollected very well the father who had worked for them, and always been kind and tried to please them. It would be but a poor return to forsake the mother he had left to their care. So they used to strap their burthen upon their backs again, and hope things would be better when their mother's health improved.

"And besides, Kate," little Ruby would say,

with her pug nose dreadfully swollen with crying, which made her look anything but pretty, "papa knows all about it, and he will love us all the more when we go to him."

You see, May had been whispering this happiness into Ruby's ears; and that father, looking down upon his "babies," saw their struggle, and as his little Ruby said, "loved them all the more."

"What are you doing in the dark?" asked Mrs. Calvert, rather sharply.

"Nothing, mamma; I have been playing, and Ruby has been warming herself, I believe."

"And you leave everything to me; but it has always been the same. I have had all to do; you don't know you're born, either of you."

"I am sorry, mamma, that I did not come to make tea."

"Ah, you'll think of it, when I am gone. I shall have spasms to-night, Kate; I feel them coming on."

Neither Kate nor Ruby made any response to this communication ; it was no use, since she had made up her mind to have spasms, spasms she would have. Once Ruby got into terrible disgrace by enquiring at " What o'clock they were to commence ?" Mrs. Calvert walked out of the room, Kate and Ruby following, to partake of the tea about which there had been a slight passage at arms.

" The old women had been busy plucking their geese " all day for the first time that season. The ground was covered with pure fluffy snow, while the trees looked as though someone had been sugaring them. Uncle Durill and Aunt May had been having a sham fight with the children, much to the amusement of all beholders, and the profound contempt of Miss Lois and Mr. Crispin in particular. They had nothing to do but sit by the fire. Lois's time hung especially heavily on her hands in consequence of Ted

Archer having gone up to town for the day on business. But the next best thing to having him to talk to, was to talk about him, and she did not know anyone so likely to pick that bone with her as Crispin. He had come into the room without any purpose, and finding Lois there had stayed. Presently he had been attracted to the window by little shrill shrieks of delight which heralded the beginning of the "great battle," and he was still lolling against the shutter with a half smile on his lips watching Evelyn, who stamped about with her sturdy little red legs and cheeks trying to catch Durill, who dodged her in the bushes. She was quite out of breath, and tumbled round with her little fists full of snow, but at last, finding she was getting the worst of it, the small tyrant commanded Uncle Durill to " 'toop down," and coolly tossed the two little cakes of snow into his face, which of course stuck in his beard and moustache, whereupon she set up another yell of delight, and called Aunty May and Ivo to look what she had done.

"I wonder how Durill has the patience to play with those children," remarked Crispin, as he returned to his seat by the fire.

He did not know that Durill had cut short his ride on purpose to please those same children.

"So do I, and as for May she is absurd over them. I never expected they would keep it up, but they do, and positively seem to grow fonder of them each day."

"Yes, the children don't trouble you much, Lois, I must say, or me either," added Crispin, with a laugh.

"Well, dear me, it is not everyone that would make the fuss about them May and Durill do; the children may well like them. Why, it was only the other night I went into the nursery to see May, and found Durill actually playing 'little piggies' with Evelyn's toes!"

"Indeed! Twenty minutes to four—it is almost time I got the trap ready, and went to the station to fetch Archer."

"Yes, it is. Will Mr. Archer remain long, Crispin?"

Crispin was in the middle of a long yawn, so Lois had to wait till he got his mouth shut.

"Stay long? I really don't know—most likely not—his cousin will want him."

"His cousin, who is he?"

"It is not a 'he' at all, it is a 'she,' and an uncommon pretty girl she is too."

"What is her name, and how do you know she is so pretty?"

Crispin stretched his neck.

"I had no idea your bump of curiosity was so largely developed, Lois. In reply to your first question her name is Aggie Russell, and the way I know she is pretty is because Ted told me so, and showed me her carte."

" Crispin, don't you think it would be polite to invite him to stay a little longer, and I will poke mamma up about those parties?"

" Possibly, but I don't expect he will. But what do you want to keep him for, Lois?"

" I want to keep him? How can you be so ridiculous, Crispin? I only thought he has had so little enjoyment since he came that it might be as well to give him a taste before he goes, so that he may retain a pleasant remembrance of us."

" Us; I like that. Ah! ah! I see the motive, Lois. But I'll tell you a secret, sister mine, it is ' no go,' so you had better not waste your valuable time."

Crispin's tone of derision cut Lois to the quick, and tears mounted to the pretty eyes, while she proceeded to defend herself.

" Cris, you are a disagreeable fellow. I hope you will bring no more of your friends here. I

only want to be civil to the man, and you immediately turn it into something else." Lois
gathered up her dress as if to rise.

" Stay a moment, Lois, I want to say something to you. You have been flirting away with
Archer ever since he came, so don't pretend you
haven't; but this time you have found your
match, young lady. There is not a bigger flirt
than Ted Archer in England; I'll back he'll not
make you an offer if he stays here six months,
and if ever he marries it will be his cousin, Miss
Agnes Russell. Now I am off to the station.
I'll ask him to stay, but after what I have told
you, I don't suppose you'll care to remind Madam
about the parties."

With a sly laugh, Crispin swung himself out
of the room, and slammed the door to.

He was delighted to have discovered Lois'
little plot, it made him feel so superior, now that

he had a rod to hold over her head, and his face beamed again as he walked to the court yard.

Lois had not a particularly long head, but after Crispin's departure something very important seemed to have possession of her nearly addled brain, for her eyes were fixed, and the smooth fingers twined themselves amongst the yellow hair. But that did not help to solve the problem, for, starting up, she stamped, and the tears again rushed to her eyes.

"I wish the man had never come near the place. I wonder why on earth Crispin could not have told that about his cousin before? Minnie will be sure to laugh, and mamma thought it would be such a capital match, and I—"

A shower of tears drowned the end of the angry beauty's speech. Poor Lois! you had played with fire once too often, and got your fingers burnt this time!

CHAPTER X.

"MAY, do you know Lois has gained the day?"

"Gained the day, Judy? What do you mean, I don't understand?"

"Why, we are to have a party before Mr. Archer goes, and that reminds me I think we ought to have new dresses, May. Mamma does not like to see us in the same things too often. What shall you get?"

May lifted her head out of the cupboard.

"What are you saying, Judy, new dresses?"

"I don't believe you have listened to me, May."

"Well, not very carefully," laughed May. "But I beg your pardon, Judy; if you will kindly repeat it I will pay more attention. Only I am so bothered, I can't find Rugg's bill. Durill has lost it, and it must be paid to-morrow. I can't bear having such a lot of things about, it makes me fidgetty. Well, go on, please, Judy; what about the dresses?"

" Why, I suppose we must get new ones; what will you have?"

" Black."

" Nonsense, May; you have heaps of black dresses, you can't have another."

" Oh, yes I can. I shall not go to much expense, either. I shall tell them to make me a stylish black grenadine, to wear with one of my low black silks. It is really a great nuisance; I wish Lois would get married and leave us in peace."

Judy smiled.

" I have a notion these parties are with that object."

" Is that so? Well, then, I shall submit with a better grace, and perhaps put a little colour on my dress if it will hasten the process."

" I am afraid it won't, May; they will be so taken up with each other that they will never notice you."

" Indeed! How wonderfully polite you are, Miss Judy. And pray who are asked to this show?"

" I don't know; I don't suppose it is decided yet. I left Lois and Crispin making out the list, which will have to be shown to mamma. There is to be no dancing, but ' coffee at half-past seven.' "

" And carriages at eleven, I suppose," chimed in Durill, who had entered just in time to catch the close of Judy's sentence. " What's it all about?"

" A party, Durill, at which you are to be

I 5

dressed as a Scotchman, and dance the ' Highland Fling' for the amusement of the audience. I fancy I see you." And they went off in a roar of laughter.

" A party ! One of those nondescript affairs ; coffee at half-past seven, indeed ! Such rubbish; the person who invented that fashion ought to be banished. I shall impose banishment upon myself for that evening. It is Lois' notion, of course ? And when is it to come off?"

" They have not decided yet ; soon, I believe ; at any rate before Mr. Archer goes."

" Humph ! That will be never, according to my reckoning ; he seems to like his quarters."

" Yes, so I think ; but I am determined of one thing, since this party is to come off (I should have said parties, for I believe this is only the beginning of a series), I will see the lists each time and suggest any alterations I think proper. I have not forgotten that awful party at which

I was victimised by the Rev. Mr. Booth. Do you recollect, May ?"

" Oh dear yes. Poor Judy ! I felt for you.".

The Rev. Mr. Booth alluded to was the curate, one of those thin limp curates that always seem a necessary appendage to a fat old rector. The Rev. James Booth (or Bottle, as Durill called him once, soon after he was imported) was a particularly lean young man, straight up and straight down, thereby raising a question in Julius Drever's mind, as to " How that fellow kept his clothes on?" The reverend gentleman had a great aptitude for asking most astonishing riddles, and when no one could or would guess them, informing the company in general that he was extremely fond of " light cakes." In fact, he was highly suggestive of a " light cake" himself, as what there was of him was particularly " flabby and dabby," and looked very much in need of a little " baking."

The dreadful ordeal she had passed through at the hands of the above-mentioned gentleman seemed to have returned to Judy's mind with double force, for she left the room at once to inspect the list, and scratch out his name if it chanced to be there.

" May, have you found that bill ?"

" No, not yet; I can't imagine where you have put it; but it must be in one of those drawers."

" I forgot to tell you I met your friend Ruby Calvert the other day, and she sent her love to you."

" Did she?   Dear little Ruby ! where did you see her ?"

" On the Dorking Road ; she looked very pretty."

" Well, don't look so serious about it, Durill !" exclaimed May, who was watching him rather narrowly.

He laughed.

"See, it is all gone; only a passing cloud, little May. But I am certain you cannot see if you put your hand on Rugg's bill; it is getting quite dark, so bundle the things in, and talk to me a bit."

Durill pulled two chairs to the fire, and sat down on one. May took the other, saying—

"This seems always my time to be idle, it used to be so at school, only we used to sit on the rug. Moments of idleness between light and darkness; someone calls it ' The children's hour.' I like that expression, don't you ?"

"Yes, May ; and that someone is Longfellow. Le says—

> "'I have you fast in my fortress,
>   And will not let you depart,
>   But put you down into the dungeon—
>   In the round tower of my heart !
>
> ' And there I will keep you for ever :
>   Yes, for ever and a day !
>   Till the walls shall crumble to ruin,
>   And moulder in dust away !'

" I have got you down there, May, though you are not a child."

" And am I all alone, Durill? I don't think I should like a dungeon quite by myself."

" No, you are not alone, May; there's a very small person with you."

" Who is it, Durill?"

" No; I cannot tell you, May."

" Why not?"

" Because, perhaps she would not like to be down in my dungeon. She may be there against her will, so I sha'n't tell anyone till I find out whether she likes it."

" And if she does not like it, will you let her out?"

" No, May; I will keep her there—

'Till the walls shall crumble to ruin,
And moulder in dust away.'"

" Cruel Durill! how unkind of you! But you might tell me who it is."

" So I will some day, May. May, don't think me a wicked fellow, but do you suppose that God has to do with all our affairs ?"

" Yes, certainly, to a great extent. We are responsible for our own actions, but He knows what we are about to do, and very often He puts us in a difficult position purposely, to try us."

" Do you think that He has to do with love ? I mean with our falling in love ?"

" Yes. There is no true love that God is absent from. He has to do with everything."

" Then why does He take our loved ones away sometimes, because, seeing all, He must know how necessary they are to us ?"

" Because He does not choose that anyone or anything should be of more consequence to you than Himself. He will not let his people make idols ; so don't you go and make an idol of that small creature you keep in your dungeon, else may be He will take her from you."

" Surely not, May,—surely not ; at least, not before we have had a little time together. He would not take my darling from me for ever ! If that came to pass, May, I don't think I should believe in ' His tender mercy ' and ' loving kindness ' again !"

" Hush, Durill ! hush ! don't say that. Why it would be out of ' tender mercy ' He would take her. Is not a mother kind who takes a sharp knife out of her child's hand. An idol is a sharp knife, for it severs the chain that binds you to God, and so you lose your inheritance. So He will take your idol away, and compel you to draw near unto Himself by means of that idol. It will act as a magnet, and you will follow after your lost darling till you reach Heaven, as the shepherds did after the star in the East, till they found the ' baby cradled in a manger.' Therefore, bereaved ones should never lose sight of those who are gone before ; they should never let go of the 'golden cord' which dangles from the clouds. Each dear one is a cord unto Heaven, stepping-stones unto everlasting glory. You speak of your darling being taken 'for ever.' It would not be for *ever*, if God did take her. He would only put her safely away on a high shelf, and you would find her there when you went!"

"But, May, when we see them laid in their graves, they are lost *to us, we* shall never have any more intercourse or companionship with them!"

"Oh! Durill, how miserable you must be with that idea in your head. Poor fellow! Do you think we are all going to be strangers in heaven? Do you think that fathers and mothers, sisters and brothers, husbands and wives, will stand next to each other and not know one another? What a horrible notion? to die, and so part from all we love, to leave our dear ones for ever—for eternity! That is an impossibility.

Why, would God have given us homes and relations, and let us love them, if he intended to divide us suddenly some day, and take us all away by ourselves? Are we not told that God's works are everlasting? Therefore, Love must be lasting, for it is one of them. Do you think we are to stand up there for ever and ever, without being nearer to those dear ones whom God took to himself so early? I cannot see that there would be any happiness in that—I should be wretched if I thought it, and dread very much the idea of dying. Who could get reconciled to the notion that when we get to heaven we should be—alone? Think for a moment—for ever alone! If such were the case, how could death be a gain? And yet we are told that it is. When God calls for first one and then another, we should not regard them as gone for *ever*—they are only lost to us until such time as we shall join them. They belong to us just the same up there as they did down here. Our Father does not wish us to look upon death as a dreadful calamity. Take, for instance, our worldly belongings—don't we prize some of them very highly, and seek to keep them from harm—put them in a drawer, and lock them up? But we know where they are, we know that by taking the key we can open that drawer and look at them. And we do not say, 'I have lost such and such a thing!' Now, that is precisely what our Father does with some of his precious ones—He takes them and puts them in a place of safety—He locks them up out of the reach of grief, pain, sickness, and want. But He tells us where we shall find the key. And having found that key, we have nothing to do but wait, and in God's good time we shall be summoned to the 'golden gate,' which will be opened to let us in—you and me, Durill—and we shall find there our treasures that God took into His safe keeping, and they will not be locked from us ever again ?"

Some redhot cinders dropped out of the grate and broke the silence. Durill sat with his eyes steady, he was realizing the truth of what May said. Presently he murmured—

" You and me, Durill ! Yes, May, child," and he took her wee hand, " we'll try to knock at that gate together, but I think I shall be obliged to hold on by the hem of your garments to reach it !" and he sighed a great big sigh.

May smiled a tender, loving smile at the great man who was trusting to her to lead him.

" Durill, you don't need me, for does not the Lord say to us each separately, ' When thou passest through the waters *I* will be with thee ; and through the rivers they shall not overflow thee.' So that you are safe if you only believe, you see !'"

" How pleased you seem, May, are you quite sure you are safe ? "

" Yes—why Durill," and the calm face turned to him confidently, " Who shall separate us from the love of Christ? Oh, who indeed? What a challenge! Neither kings, queens, noblemen, nor statesmen, can interfere between Christ and one of His children."

" May, you are showing me my weakness— my blindness, child."

" Well, the Lord won't let you be blind long, Durill; he'll take you by the hand soon, and guide you."

Durill gazed at the still face, with the firelight dancing on it, and the thought crossed his mind, " Surely the Lord has taken you by the hand." May was the first to break the silence.

" It must be very late; the dressing bell will be sounding soon. Come, Durill."

" Very well, love ; kiss me, May."

" You tyrant," laughed May, " you should ask my pleasure."

Durill stooped and fondled her, and almost carried her up the stairs that tired poor little Evelyn's fat legs so.

CHAPTER XI.

THE brothers Hardwick were both gentlemen possessing good forms and handsome faces. Captain Godwin Meredith Hardwick was the elder by ten or twelve years. He was rather like Durill Drever, but not quite so handsome, though good looking enough. His face had not such a genial look, and his eyes were more piercing, not so soft; his hair was darker, being black and almost straight, while Durill's formed itself into charming little rings and curls round his head. Both were fine, handsome men. Captain Hardwick was a little older than Durill; he had sold out of the army, and taken up his quarters at Felton Cottage. It was situated in the centre of the village, down one of those curious lanes which a stranger finds so difficult to discover, and which seem to abound in a rustic village. There was a quarry close to, all over-grown with bushes and trees, and by following the narrow path, only protected by a crippled rail, you came out at the side of the village inn.

The place was a perfect "maze;" it had no less than six entrances, with lanes branching off, but whichever you took you invariably landed at the quarry. In truth, it was just a ring, with pretty little nests round, and the old quarry in the middle. But it was very charming; being slightly elevated, you commanded a good view of the roofs of the old-fashioned cottages with the pigeons clustering round the chimneys. There in the early morning during the hot summer months you would see the pretty village en-veloped in a haze, which gradually cleared off as the sun rose to assert his superiority, and flashed his scorching rays upon the parched earth. Then the cocks would commence to crow and the cows to low, and one by one the kitchen chimneys belonging to each cottage would emit a faint curl of blue smoke, as the village awoke to the business of the day.

There, in the still winter's night, when the ground lay covered with snow, and the trees were wrapped each in a mantle of white, the moon would shed forth its glorious light, which seemed to be but the reflection of God's face in its purity, and through the long still night keep watch over the sleeping village.

It would see each candle put out, and knees bent, while girlish lips asked in simple words for protection and God's blessing on themselves and those they loved. Later on, when it took another peep into the small rooms, it would see the occupants sleeping sweetly with their young faces turned towards the friendly light, while a much-loved name or tender word dropped from their smiling lips, or a happy tear glittered like a diamond on the long lashes. And the moon-beams, stealing softly to them, would kiss and bathe their faces in its silvery light, then glide away, wishing that " Love's young dream " was not so short, and leave them sleeping!

One day the tranquility of Felton Cottage had been broken into by the arrival of George Henry Hilton Hardwick, the Captain's younger brother, a wild, handsome, spoilt fellow— lieutenant in a dashing Highland regiment. Both were extravagant, but George, having the advantage of his elder brother for example, soon reflected great credit upon his teacher, and passed him. Then the Captain commenced to remon-strate gently with the spoilt fellow, whom he regarded with the most fatherly affection, and considered a boy.

Their father had died, leaving young George a legacy to his big brother. Captain Godwin Hardwick was the next heir to a title and estate, and failing him George came in for it.

But it seemed an unconscionable long time coming to those two gentlemen. Their uncle was very tenacious.

George was stretched full length on the sofa in their pretty sitting-room, smoking, and occasionally relieving the monotony by singing snatches of the last new comic songs. The Captain regarded the dear boy attentively for a few seconds, with his long, supple limbs, as lithe as an Indian's—in fact, there was no telling how much Indian blood there was not in Master George, for they were but half-brothers—and George had been born out in India, where it was said his mother died, poor lady! leaving to her husband a little wiry baby, with a particularly

dark skin, and a pair of the largest brilliant
black eyes possible. He was wonderfully like
an Indian in complexion, eyes, and hair, also in
his flexibility of body. Lying there, full length
on his back (which, by the way, seemed to be a
favourite position of his), he was a pleasing
picture to behold, in his uncommon beauty.

Captain Hardwick appeared satisfied with his
survey, when he said, in the mildest tone possible—

"George, don't shout quite so loudly."

George's reply was to languidly turn his head,
and flash a blinding look out of his black eyes at
his elder brother. George was always "so tired,"
but he could rouse up to some purpose at times.
He was particularly attached to the Captain,
whom he always spoke of as "my brother."

Both the Hardwicks had a wonderfully low-
toned voice when speaking, which contrasted

somewhat oddly with their warrior-like appearance. Presently George roused himself and confronted his brother.

" Godwin, when are you going to see about getting me a move on?"

" A move on? Oh! a step higher. Well, soon, George. But, really, you have been so extravagant lately, George, that I must see what is to be got."

George flung his long legs about, and muttered—

" Bother the money," and something about a "long-winded old gentleman," who, in all probability, was his venerable uncle. George asked his brother mildly—

" Are you going to this party at Wild Wood?"

" Yes, I suppose so; it is so awfully slow there is nothing for a fellow to do here. Are you?"

" Certainly. I met Durill, and he said it would not be very enjoyable he was afraid—but I shall chance that."

George suddenly got animated.

"I wonder whether the Calverts are going? I say, Godwin, do you know?"

"Know what, George?" inquired the Captain, who had the patience of Job with him.

"Why, whether the Calverts are going, to be sure?"

"No, I don't; but I think it most probable."

"Then I shall go. Here, where's the ink?— give me some paper Godwin—look sharp!"

"You will find all you want in that drawer," replied his much enduring brother.

The pen sputtered under George's frantic strokes, and at last the note was ready, and George rose and intimated his intention of going out. No doubt the Captain was rather glad to be rid of him, for he returned to his easy chair with a sigh of satisfaction.

He was settled down now, and enjoyed the quiet of the pretty village. He had been rather like George once, though not quite so mad, but he had dashed and flashed about a good deal in his time. But like all fast men he arrived at the end of the string too soon, and found a good piece of ground on the other side to be walked over, and it is not pleasant to walk alone, therefore he wished to have a companion who would be as "a light unto his path," till such a time as he might reasonably expect to be called to his fathers.

George went along indolently, as was his wont, and after posting the note, turned into the "Stork," and electrified the waiter by asking him "What he thought of the internal policy of Japan?"

"Sir?" exclaimed the astonished waiter.

"Oh! never mind, it will do another day—it is of no consequence."

To his friends he would remark—

"I think the people in this village consider me mad—my brother says he is sure of it."

And not much wonder either if they did.

The night of the hated party at Wild Wood came all too soon to please some of its occupants, and May was as good as her word, and at six o'clock was attiring herself at express speed in the promised black gauze. She was fastening the band round her not too small waist, as Judy entered, ready dressed.

Miss Drever had treated herself to a new garment, a rich purple silk trimmed with white duchess lace. It was a handsome dress, and suited her remarkably well. She swept up to May with her staid walk and inspected her rather critically. But May stood the scrutiny well; though she had but a black dress on it was good, the silk thick, and the gauze fine. Her well-shaped shoulders and arms showed through it, and the black imparted a whiter look to her skin. She was well put together and not too short, while her bearing gave her a decidedly striking appearance. The glass reflected back a pale, calm face, nay, a fine, handsome, intelligent face, with its speaking eyes and determined mouth, which, when she smiled, gave her very much the look of handsome Durill. May was always considered the plainest of the Drever family, but only by those who were short of discernment. What beauty May had would last for ever—she had beauty of mind and a peaceful conscience. There were two or three who would have been only too glad to have taken stately, calm May by the hand and placed her at the head of their table.

Judy smiled as she looked at May; perhaps she was aware that she, decked out in a bran new silk, at 16s. a-yard, would pass for nothing beside the calm, pale girl in plain black. May was the sort of girl that people would turn round to look twice at, and although they would not ejaculate " How beautiful !" they would ask

" Who is she ?" Over weaker minds she held wonderful control, and drove them before her like a flock of geese ; and the strong ones were fascinated by her. So that May was a dangerous opponent in the matrimonial field, when she chose to exert her powers, but that was rarely ; she scarcely ever admired a gentleman enough to devote herself entirely to his conquest. Even when talking agreeably to any one she only gave them one eye and ear, the other two were picking up everything that went on. Her faculties were particularly acute ; at one glance she saw all and understood it.

Judy's smile deepened, and presently she exclaimed—

" May, what a queer girl you are ; dressed all in black you look like a widow or a nun. Surely you are going to introduce some colour to relieve it ?"

" Now, Judy, just have patience ; wait till you

have seen the others. They are sure to be
dazzling, so that before the evening is over many
people will thank me for putting on this black
dress to rest their eyes."

" But why not put a little colour?"

" So I intend to."

She opened a draw and took out some cases
containing jewellery, all dead gold, perfectly
plain but exceptionally good. These she put on,
and turning to Judy asked, " There, is that
better?"

" Yes, a great improvement, but—"

A rap at the door stopped Judy's remark. May
opened it. There stood Blake, a splendid red
rose in one hand and a small box in the other.

" Mr. Durill has sent you these, Miss May,
with his love, and will you please to wear the
rose to-night?"

" Ah! yes. How kind of Durill. Thank you,
Blake."

May put the lovely flower down, and Judy took it up.

"What a beauty! I wonder where Durill got it; we have not one out yet. I heard Lois asking King only this afternoon. I suppose he got it in London. Covent Garden, most likely."

May did not reply; she was gazing at the contents of the mysterious box brought by Blake. There on a bed of soft white wool reposed a small thing that glittered and danced, winked with its brilliant eyes, and shot forked fire from its red mouth.

Judy came up, and, standing, looked over her shoulder. Her breath was all gone, but the first use she made of it when it returned was to give vent to one deeply-breathed "Oh!" which spoke volumes.

"How splendid!" said May, her face beaming with pleasure, as she tenderly lifted the wicked serpent so cunningly coiled into a ring out of its snowy bed, and slipped it on to one of her pretty short finge rs.

" Yes it is, indeed, splendid ! How fortunate you are, May ! Durill never tires of giving you pretty things ; and no wonder, you are his right hand in nearly everything."

Judy felt very proud of her young sister, who seemed to have been sent to help them all with her fresh young brains, common sense, and loving heart.

The old Squire always made a point of calling for May when anything was amiss, and it had become to them all quite natural now, though when first she came into notice Judy did not quite like it. But then May was so quiet, and took upon herself no airs, always seemed to have plenty to do, able to amuse herself, never felt lonely or depressed, or pushed herself forward.

All this helped to make the hold she had got already firmer, and little May, with her paltry twenty years, was appealed to and respected by everyone, from the Squire to the youngest servant. The older ones—Mrs. Morrison, the housekeeper, Blake, and old Nurse Joyce—looked upon Miss May as something out of the common, and decidedly above the average. Nurse Joyce used to inform them in the servants' hall—

" *That* blessed lamb gave me no trouble—*never*."

" Now, May, here's your rose, pin it in."

" Which side, Judy ?"

" The left, I suppose ; at any rate, you cannot be far wrong, if any, for that is generally where Minnie and Lois put theirs."

May did it, perhaps a little awkwardly, but at any rate naturally. And the mirror showed a

very nice girl, indeed, according to Judy's notion.
Suddenly there was a fluttering at the door, and
something floated into the room radiant and
dazzling. It was the beauty Lois, bewitching in
a wonderful work of art called a dress. It was
pale green tulle, tucked, frilled, and flounced,
with white; it had come from Regent Street that
day in a wooden box smothered in silk paper.
But, dreadful to relate, Madam Rento had made
it rather too tight for the trim little waist, and
Lois came fluttering in, her pretty face all awry,
and her mouth pinched like a baby's when it is
on the point of affording someone the privilege
of testing the power of its infantine lungs.

"Oh, May, do try and pull me to; Parker cannot manage it, clumsy thing, and Demont is with
mamma."

She wisked round and displayed to Judy and
May a good wide breach that the dress would not
stride over.

"It wants a steady pull, May; do try, there's a good girl!"

Judy looked at May in consternation.

"Yes, I will try, Lois; but the dress is made too small. However came Madame Rento to make such a mistake?"

"Oh, it is not her fault. It was Minnie, who said I ought to make my waist smaller, and I ordered Madame Rento to do so; but she might have used her own judgment."

"No; if that be the case, the fault is your own, not Madame Rento's. Come a trifle nearer, please, Lois."

May pulled with all her might, and the poor dress cracked and started; but it came to, to the infinite joy of Lois, who showered thanks without number upon May, who was occupied attentively regarding the tips of her fingers, which smarted considerably.

Lois walked to the glass, put it back as far as

possible, and commenced that peculiar dance
that ladies are so often engaged in when they
desire to see how their train hangs, and have
only a short glass. I really don't think there can
be a more aggravating thing than a fruitless
endeavour to see your own back. There you go,
prancing about, so intent upon seeing, that if the
room be not particularly large, you in all probability run the off-side of your face against something hard, and are rudely reminded that there
are more things in the world than the set of your
skirt, or that your cheek-bones must be very
prominent. Lois was just now occupied in this
said dance, and May and Judy regarding her
with no little amazement. Really, it required
everyone to look twice before they could be quite
sure what they saw. The small figure, the shim-
mering hair that looked as though it had gold-
dust sprinkled over it, the bewitching eyes, and,

last but not least, the united efforts of Madame Rento and her assistants, the wonderful green and white dress. While looking at this vision, your mind hovered between a princess in a fairy tale, a spirit, and one of those lovely creatures that spend ten weeks of their existence during the winter nightly swung up in gilt a basket, or appearing in a cloud out of the sea, riding on a pearl shell at Covent Garden or Drury Lane. But it was, you found out at the second look, Lois Benton Drever, only marvellously "got up."

Unobserved by the three, Durill had entered, and immediately became transfixed by the figure before the mirror.

" Bless me !" he ejaculated, at last, which proclaimed his presence.

And May went forward to thank him for his presents.

" Don't mention it, darling ; you know you

would not have another Gipsy, so I thought I would give you something that no one could ride to death. But how nice you look!"

And he held her at arm's length, to get a better view, then kissed her fondly. The "Bless me!" was intended for Lois, and he followed it up by saying—

"Really, you petrified me, Lois! You should give us timely notice when you intend transforming yourself into a gauze balloon, so that we might come prepared for the astonishing sight. Well, if you don't achieve the grand object to-night, and carry all before you I *shall* be surprised. The man must be iron that could resist that garment, without taking into consideration the time and expense required to put it together. When I am engaged, if my young lady does not get herself up like that I shall take it as a mark of great disrespect. Only I should be compelled to admire her at a distance, my arms not being

long enough to reach. No one could get within
two yards of you, Lois; you put me in mind of
those pen-wipers they had at the bazaar last
year. I bought one, and positively I find black
and red cloth ladies' petticoats most useful!"

Judy and May were both shaking; it was
quite a picture to behold big Durill standing
there looking as handsome as paint, with a
comical twinkle in his eye, and Lois spread out
like a ship in full sail, and every hair bristling
with anger.

"Durill, you are positively insulting; you are
most ignorant; you cannot understand or appreciate anything. This dress was copied from one
worn by the Countess of Perth at a ball last
week. The only difference being that mine has
no real lace and flowers. It is a sweet thing."

Durill made a courtly bow.

"You resisted the flowers and real lace! You
astonish me. Well, it is a sweet thing!"

Lois had tact enough to see that Durill was on the eve of laughing, so she made her escape from the room. And a happy thing she did, for no sooner had the tip of the six yards behind, called a train, vanished, than he gave way, and, in company with Judy and May, laughed heartily.

"'Pon my word, Lois is a caution! The idea of getting herself up so strong. If Minnie has done likewise, there will be no moving about. Why did you not put on something like hers, May?"

" The idea, Durill! Imagine plain me attired like a fairy princess! My skin's too muddy, and my arms too fleshy. Those things would not set on me."

" Well, I am not so sure about that; it seems to me they would sit anywhere, providing you put bustle enough under them. But I like you very much better as you are, ' my lady.' "

" Don't call me ' my lady,' pray."

" Why not ? you are very fitted to be one."

" Nonsense ; are you trying to make me conceited ? If so you have commenced rather late in the day ; I have had too many opportunities of looking at myself in the glass."

" No, I am not wishful to make you vain, and I could not if I tried ; but don't abuse yourself, May. Though your skin is not too clear, there is plenty of white under it, and it contrasts very well with your hair and eyes."

He was leaning his great body against the wall staring at May, who stood with a highly amused expression before him. Judy was sitting near the toilet table smiling.

" May, you make me feel frightfully aged ; you, the child, and looking so old. It is a good thing I don't care about getting married, for I stand a very poor chance when you are pointed at as the youngest. You are getting quite worn looking, May."

" Worn looking ! Surely not. But I think you are right, too, Judy ; she does look old. You are worn with the care of others, May, love."

" No, Durill, I am not, only we dark Drevers always age sooner than the light ones."

" Age ! who talks of age at twenty ?"

" I do. I left twenty years behind me long ago, according to my own feelings. Only somebody awoke me one morning and told me I was twenty that day."

" Ah !" sighed Judy, " some people do feel older than others. But wait till you are my age, and then talk about ageing."

Miss Drever rose and announced her opinion that it was time they went down.

" All right, Judy ; go along, we'll follow. Come, May."

He took her on his arm, and they went along, saying clever things to each other and laughing. They enjoyed each other's society ; it rested them.

CHAPTER XII.

By twos and threes the people arrived, and located themselves according to their taste. In one corner sat little Ruby Calvert, in white muslin dotted with blue. Pretty she looked, little thing; and Crispin seemed to think so, for he was chattering into one small ear very earnestly. She half listened and smiled, now and then saying a few words, but her eyes were roving over the large room. She wanted to find something, and she ought to have been able to, for it was by no means a little thing. What lovely eyes they were; they can be best described in the words of De Musset—

"Sweeter eyes in this world were never made
To scan blue heavens and reflect their shade."

The object she was in search of was at the end of the room, lolling over a couch, talking polite rubbish to a decidedly smitten lady, with at least five pounds' worth of somebody else's hair on her head, and a camelia twisted in on the very top as large as a cabbage. Whenever she bent there was a very ominous creak, which brought back to Durill's mind the fate of a rather sloppily made young lady who was present at a social gathering at Mrs. Calvert's one evening. She came attired in a white skirt and black velvet short bodice, and about eight yards of tartan plaid broad ribbon, which was twisted in a wonderful manner, under her arms, over them, across her chest, round her waist, and eventually formed a sash behind. A roller towel would have looked just as graceful, and have answered the purpose better, that of pulling her together into something like shape. She rejoiced in one of those figures that are the bane of poor dressmakers' existence. She was like a badly stuffed doll, too limp; she wanted more bran and a stitch putting through each limb, they hung as if on a thread. While sitting at supper every one was startled by a sudden wrench and explosion, and an immense pin flew violently to the other side of the room. Without the least assistance the sash (or more correctly the binder) slowly unwound itself, and Miss Bridget got as red as a poppy. Kate Calvert and a few more kind young ladies offered their aid, and with the help of several pins they got her together again, much to the amusement of the rest. Possibly it was the exertion of eating that caused her to burst, or more probably singing " The Lover and the Bird," which she considered she did to per-fection.

The fate of big Miss Bridget rose vividly to the memory of Durill, and he thought how extremely inconvenient it would be if one of the merry cracks the lady of the cabbage camelia was giving should end in an explosion. But he resolved to stand his ground till he really saw something alarming, and then depart. At no great distance from him sat Kate Calvert, May, and the two Hardwicks, and scraps of their conversation kept reaching his ear from time to time.

"Do you frequently go to London, Captain Hardwick?"

"Yes, about twice a week now, since George has been with me; he is so restless. But it seems rather strange to have myself called Captain Hardwick. I dropped it when I left the army. I don't care about it on account of those skippers, you know."

"Ah, then I will remember in future," replied May, "but I am used to hearing you called so by Durill."

" I like it well enough when you use it, only it would be a nuisance to be taken for a skipper."

George turned his brilliant eyes.

" So Godwin is giving you a lesson, Miss May?"

" Well, not quite that, only stating his dislikes and likes."

" And Mr. George is telling me that he is getting weary of Maldon."

" Well, you see, Miss Calvert, it is all very well for my brother, but for me it is awfully slow. And I am certain the people think me mad, my brother says he is sure of it."

" How is that?"

" Why, I like a little fun; and no one knows me down here, you know, and so I don't care. When we were at Perth we used to have such fun. I was turned out of the Concert Room in the Town Hall there for making a noise. We used to go on purpose to upset the audience, you know."

"I am afraid you are a bad character, Mr. Hardwick."

"Do you really think so?" and the black eyes flashed unutterable things at little rosy Kate, who sat very demurely, looking very bewitching in a blue silk with white muslin over.

Durill came up then, saying, "They are clammering for more music, would you favour us, Miss Calvert?"

"Oh, yes, with pleasure, Mr. Drever."

The people opened their ears when Kate Calvert commenced, and George Hardwick admired both the player and the playing. Big Durill found his way to Ruby, and began to entertain her very successfully. Ruby looked quite content to have it go on for ever, and Durill forgot the existence of the rest.

They talked of a wood where violets grew, with

the river dancing through it, where someone went
fishing for trout.　It was quite close to home; it
was natural they should speak of it.　They loved
every wood and old gate.　They each stood on a
separate path, but they ran side by side; they
would journey together for company, and if a
brook crossed their path, strong Durill would lift
Ruby over it.　God has made those two paths to
meet at the end, but it is a long road, night will
overtake them by the way.　Supposing they get
divided?　What then?　Ah! they will turn about
with a dull pain at their hearts, and retrace their
steps through the wood, looking amid the tangled
brushwood for each other.　But they will not be
able to call out for fear anyone should hear
them, and ask them what they had lost.　They
could not tell.　How did they know that the two
roads met at the end, they had got out of the
track.　How could they tell that the angels were
crying over them because they were weary

wanderers, and had no place to rest. God help all seekers in that wood !

A day or two after the party, Judy and May were talking to Lois, who had come into the nursery. May was getting some things ready for the children's dressmaker. Ivo was to be promoted into knickerbockers, and May and Judy did not quite agree about the length of the legs. Judy wanted them to be a shade below the knee, but May was determined that Ivo's should only extend half way down the thigh—that there should be a lace ruffle, at least to the velvet ones.

"Why, Judy, the child has such splendid legs it would be a shame to hide them; and besides, it is more *distingué*. What with his curls and lace frills he will look like a young prince."

"Yes, it is very true; all that I know, but he will be chilly, I am afraid."

"Not in the house; his others shall button at

the knee during the winter; what do you think, Lois?"

" Make them that way by all means.   I detest those other things, they are so dreadfully common now.   But have you heard the news?"

" News?   No; what is it?   A birth, marriage, or death?"

" Neither.   A dinner party to be given by Mr. Archer on Thursday night at the Stork.   A bachelors' affair, of course;   it is very kind of him, is it not?"

" Kind!   Well, I don't know; I suppose it suits his purpose."

" There you are again, Judy, forever ready to have a pick at some one."

" Not at all, Lois, only I really don't see any-thing kind about it ; if he had taken himself off a little sooner it would have been far kinder, according to my opinion."

Lois' cheeks were scarlet.

" Whatever do you mean by that, Judy? Surely mamma can have anyone she chooses here without any interference from you."

" Lois, Lois," said May, gently.

" I don't care, May; it is no use Loising me. I shall speak out when I have a mind to. Judy is always damping all our little pleasures, just because she is too old to care about them herself. I suppose you are angry that we have come out of our shells once or twice since Mr. Archer has been here, and had a few parties."

" Lois, you know perfectly well it is nothing of the kind. That my reason for wishing he had gone concerns one person alone, and that person is yourself."

May lifted her head in astonishment, and turned to Lois.

" Surely we are not going to have a second edition of Charles Blacket, Lois? Have you forgotten what papa said to you about that? Pray are you engaged to this Archer?"

" No."

" Engaged!" exclaimed Judy, " I should think not. May, if you had seen and heard what I did in the conservatory last night you would not ask that. I am heartily ashamed of you, Lois, to behave as you have done. You foolish girl, could you not see that he was just amusing himself at your expense in that cool, gentlemanly way of his, pretending to make love to you and *sneering* all the time. I may well wish he had gone sooner, but I do hope while he is here that you will content yourself with ordinary politeness."

The bubble had burst before the conceited Lois' eyes, and like the generality of weak girls, she commenced to cry like a baby, and by gasps upbraid Judy as a mean thing to act the spy.

" Act the spy, indeed! There was not much spying about it. Mr. Archer knew I was there if you did not, because we looked at each other. The trees are not so high as all that. And he has a pretty good idea of what I think of him too. But I can't and don't blame him; men are all alike, and like to have their vanity fed, and you made a dead set at him from the first. Fire is a dangerous thing to play with, Lois; all flirts find that out sooner or later."

" Excellent advice, Judy, but given a little bit too late. Lois is burnt already."

May looked on with a sorrowful face; presently she went up to the sobbing Lois, and said gently—

" Don't grieve, Lois; Judy won't tell; you'll get over it, and it is a lesson well learnt I see. Go and bathe your face; your eyes will be as red as ferrets' presently, and then everyone will want to know what is the matter."

Lois left the room with her handkerchief to her pretty eyes. It is not at all agreeable to find that you have been made a fool of, and Lois shed tears on that account, also because she had really taken a fancy to the gay Archer, and most determinedly banished from her mind the existence of his cousin Aggie Russell. And if she remembered it, it was only to draw comparisons and speculate whether Miss Russell was as pretty as herself. Besides, is not " possession nine points of the law ?" and had she not got him in the house, and as many opportunities of talking to him as she desired. So Lois lulled herself to sleep, and from that sleep she was rudely awakened by plain-spoken Judy. May was the first to speak as the door closed upon the figure of Lois.

" Judy, I am very sorry for this !"

" So am I, May, and what is more, I am ashamed. But, between you and me, I consider

Minnie has a great deal of the blame on her shoulders. Both she and mamma have talked and puffed Lois up. What a capital match it would be, etc., etc., till positively Lois has got to regard it as a certainty; little fool."

Judy's indignation was very natural, and May bent over the basket of little socks with a hot flush on her face. Presently she raised her clear eyes, and looked at Judy—

" I think we must be gentle, and have patience with Lois over this, Judy. I feel sorry for her, I fancy she has got to like Mr. Archer, and I am afraid it will go hardly with her, and I believe kindness will answer best. I don't fancy she will take her trouble to mamma."

" Why not, May ?"

" Well, I don't quite know, only I could not fancy anyone imparting their sorrows to mamma, least of all a sorrow like that."

" I am not surprised at that, May, you never

were a mother's girl, or I either. But Minnie and Lois were always whispering their secrets to mamma; such a pack of rubbish to!"

May laughed.

"Poor Minnie and her love passages with Mark, how often I incurred her displeasure by laughing, and then mamma used to take me to task. Bah! I am sick of love, Judy, thank heaven Lois is the last. But I am right down sorry about this Archer business."

"Being sorry won't do much good that I can see. I mean to give him a regular set down the first chance I get. Durill would do it to perfection. What do you say to telling him, May?"

"Oh! I will see about it. He is not quite ignorant of the state of affairs, Judy, because we had a talk about it when first he came."

"I might have known that. You two wise ones are always observing other people's shortcomings. But really, Lois deserves this, she *is* such an incorrigible flirt."

"I had rather she had been punished some other way though, Judy. Thank goodness to-day is Tuesday; and he goes on Friday?"

"Yes, that is a comfort. Well, I must go. Why don't you let Parker repair the children's things, May?"

"So I do, only they are so brisk they get through such a quantity; and, besides, I like to do for them, dear little things. And if I always work with my head, I shall forget how to use my hands."

"Not you, indeed. You are a good girl, May. I believe you were sent to prop us all up, and keep us in order. That calm face of yours is worth anything to us poor wavering mortals."

Judy stood looking down at May's busy fingers. May lifted her head—

"Judy, what is the matter—anything wrong with you?"

"No, May, not anything more to-day than any other day. The ghost of my old trouble comes back to me sometimes, May, that is all."

There was a sad ring in poor Judy's voice; she kept her grief bottled up, but at times the cork came out. There was a mighty old tree opposite the nursery window, and it waved its naked limbs in tune to the bleak wintry wind. Judy was very like that tree—she was there, but stripped of all her green leaves. The oak would get them again, but she never would. The sunshine of Judith Drever's life had passed away.

May laid the little stocking down, and put her hand on Judy's.

"If it does, you need not look so dismal over it, Judy. Do you know the truest safeguard against unhappy reflections is a contented, cheerful mind.

Come into this room oftener when the children are here, their society will do you good ; their minds are always so fresh, they will entice you out of the gloom."

Judy glanced at May's cheerful face. She knew she was right, but then it is hard to part with anything that one has become accustomed to. Indeed, to some people there is pleasure in brooding over and nursing their griefs—a decidedly grim pleasure. It is the same with delicate people, or, I should more properly say, hipped people, for half their ailments are fancied, and if not fancied, exaggerated. They consider themselves too weakly to do anything, consequently through the long, long day they are on the look out for some ache or pain. The least twitch is magnified into the commencement of some serious complaint, till at last they get so used to being nursed, pampered, and coddled, so used to this soothing drink and that delicate morsel, so used to take their breakfast in bed, and lie there in state till ten or half-past, till in the end they cannot get up. Then the excuse is, " I have such bad nights, I do not sleep." Not likely; they never exert either mind or body, therefore they don't want so much rest. Imagination will almost accomplish anything, and with delicate, nervous people it is always particularly vivid in conjuring up diseases. Therefore the best thing for them is to keep them constantly employed, whether they like it or not, and to procure for their companion a very unsympathetic person. Hipped people invariably begin with nothing, but they nearly always end with a great deal.

CHAPTER XIII.

" MAY, you don't know, you have not suffered as I have."

"No, that is true; but yet I cannot see that you need be miserable with it."

" Do you want him back, Judy ?"

" Oh ! no, May, indeed I don't."

" Then why do you hanker after him? You could not marry him, because he is only an aristocratic scoundrel, and if you had married him you would have been obliged to decamp from each place as it got too hot to hold you, or come back here and played the ' Cross Widow.' "

Judy slightly winced at this.

"May, you take a too practical view of the case; it is not right to reduce love in that way."

"Isn't it? It seems to me just the very thing we ought to do. Half the girls are blinded; they think it is all to be sunshine, and that food, etc., will drop from Heaven, and when they come to their senses again it is too late. I don't see how you are going to love if you don't respect, and I am certain you would not have done that when you found his true character out. No, Judy, I consider that you have had a very narrow escape from a life of wretchedness, and instead of looking upon it as a great sorrow, you ought to regard it as a special mercy."

"May, do you know where he is?"

"Yes; he is abroad living on his wits. But don't you go thinking about him any more, Judy. I would not keep a bad thing in my heart. I wonder what the Lord thinks of you, cherishing a wicked idol? Judy, be wise and put it away from you; you will be sorry some day if you don't."

"May, I cannot argue with you ; you are too far away for me, I cannot follow you. But I hear little feet pattering, so good-bye."

The children rushed into the room, quite rosy with the keen frosty air.

"Aunty May, we have had such a nice ride on Moppet. Evelyn did not want to come home."

"Indeed! Don't you care to come back to us, Evelyn ?"

"Ris," answered Evelyn, tugging at her seal-skin turban, the elastic of which had got fast in her curls. "Me like to come home; you dot a cake for Evelyn ?"

"A cake? No; tea will be up directly, darling; but you can have some bread and butter if you like. Ivo, will you take some ?"

"No, thank you, Aunty May."

Girls are generally more forward than boys in

speaking, but in this case it was not so. Ivo spoke perfectly well for his age, whereas fat little Evelyn made a dreadful mess of the Queen's English. May had arrived at the end of the holey stockings, so she put them right, and prepared to leave the nursery.

" Don't do, Aunty May ; Evelyn wants to sit on your knee."

" But I hear Parker with the tea things ; don't you want your tea, Evelyn ?"

" Ris, wid you."

" I do not want any now, dear, so get on my lap and tell me all about your ride on Moppet."

Evelyn jabbered through the account, helped out by Ivo, who stood patiently till his sister had finished. He was a a noble boy—so gentle and yet so high-spirited—he was like a young war horse when he shook his curls back. May thought there was not such another boy in the world. He was so independent, no one thought of nursing him like they did little roly poly Evelyn.

"Now you both want washing and making neat, and here is Parker waiting for you, and so you must kiss me and say good-bye for the present, darlings."

A great many hugs and kisses and May was permitted to depart, on condition that she would come and tell them a story, or that uncle Durill would give them some "pig-a-baggies" round the nursery before they went to bed.

May had made up her mind to speak to Crispin, and sound him about Mr. Archer. Poor Lois had indeed been caught, for she had confided it all to May between gasps and sobs.

"But, May, indeed I thought he was in earnest, I had no idea he was amusing himself, and I don't believe he was. It is all Judy's ill-nature."

"Lois, that is extremely foolish of you, as if Judy would mind anything about it, she only spoke for your own good."

It was no use trying to convince Lois, her senses were never too acute at the best of times, and now this little trouble had quite overturned them for the time being. So May resolved to go to work her own way. She was friends with Crispin, of course, but nothing more than mere friends. They did not suit each other; but Crispin reverenced May, nevertheless. She had shown great forbearance with him about poor Gipsy—never made the slightest difference in her manner towards him—and it had rather astonished Crispin, and raised May in his eyes. What could his narrow, mean mind make of May's superior noble one? Nothing.

Thursday evening was the dinner party at the "Stork," and May watched Crispin, and waylaid him as he was going to dress.

"Crispin, can you spare me a few moments; I want to speak to you?"

"Yes, May, certainly."

She stepped into his room with him, and closed the door. Crispin stood looking just a little uncomfortable; no one cared to be taken to task by May. She never spared them while she was about it; that sharp tongue of hers cut right and left.

"Crispin, has Mr. Archer said anything to you since he has been here, or before?"

"What about?"

"His prospects, his intentions, or his love affairs, for, I presume he is not without them?"

"Oh, no, he is not free from them—Ted flirts right and left. Look here, May, I know what has brought you here, you come on behalf of Lois. It serves her just right. I told her some time since that he loved his cousin, Miss Russell, but she is so conceited she imagines she can carry all before her. I also told her what a flirt he was, and if she put her finger in the fire after that, it was her own look out."

Crispin threw his shoulders back with a great air of gratification, and waited for May to speak.

"I did not tell you Lois had got burnt, Crispin, but my object in asking you the question was this: I have noticed how things have been going for some time, and I wanted to be convinced whether my impression of him was correct."

"And what is your impression?"

"That he is a villain."

"A villain! that is coming it too strong, May."

"Well, what do you call him?

"Call him? nothing; I cannot see why you should either."

"No; I did not expect that you would see,

Crispin; we rarely view things from the same position. I won't trespass on your time any longer; you will want to dress for the dinner."

May opened the door and walked out, leaving Crispin with an uneasy doubt in his mind as to what she meant to do. Her quiet manner and complete absence of temper had told him nothing. He was afraid of her; he knew that her brown eyes saw a great way down; and he took to wondering how she would look in a witness box. It would take a great deal to upset that self-possession of hers, it would take a clever man to baffle May, and he gave it as his private opinion—and very private it was, too seeing that it was not spoken—that it would go hard with the opposite party when May's time came. Meanwhile May thoughtfully dressed herself for the home dinner. Durill had been much engaged the last few days, and he often only had time to rush to his room before the last bell. His engineering was progressing rapidly, and he was frequently making flying visits to London. "But it will soon be settled, May, and then I can see to home duties for a bit."

Ted Archer and Crispin rattled down to the "Stork," leaving Durill to take his dinner at home, but he promised to look in later on. Lois appeared pale and heavy eyed, and made that ever convenient and much-abused excuse of a "bad headache," when questioned by Madam. Judy sat rigid and stiff, only condescending to shoot a swift glance at May. Durill, however, was too sharp, he saw it all, and partly understood, and what he did not he got May to explain to him.

"So that's it, is it? Well, it's very nice, I must say. Lois wants smacking."

"Yes, she is to blame, I know, yet I do feel just a little sorry for her; you see it is such a 'let down.' Judy blames mamma and Minnie for a great portion of it, and I believe she is quite correct."

"So do I; Minnie is a little fool, with her infernal nonsense, and the mother's not much better. I am awfully glad the fellow goes to-morrow. I don't suppose anyone will be much the wiser, unless one of us tells, and that's not very likely."

"Good gracious, Durill, no. I am ashamed of it, I can assure you. Is this party to be a late affair?"

"Most likely; when these fellows get together they seem inclined to sit for ever. Are you going to sit up for me, love?"

"If you want me to. I will keep a good fire in my dressing-room, and leave the door open, so that if I do go to bed you can warm yourself. But I shall sit up as long as I can, because I have something to do."

" That's a kind little sister. Never you get in love, May; recollect I cannot spare you."

" Well, don't squeeze me so hard, you monster, and do go, if you intend to."

" Why, your face is red! Come, Mademoiselle May, what is that for?"

" Oh! my face is red, is it? and no wonder, after the awful hug you treated me to just now; you will give me a fit some day."

Durill laughed, and turned to go.

" Durill, stay a second," called May. " The children made me promise that one of us would go and see them to-night before they went to bed. They would like you to give them a few 'pig-a-baggies' round the nursery, Durill. Do go; a little play will do them so much good."

" All right. It will do when they are in their nightgowns, won't it?"

" Yes, quite well, I dare say they will enjoy it

more too, but don't keep them out of bed too long."

"No, but you had better come, and then you can guard your chicks."

"I'll see."

About a quarter of an hour after the most extraordinary sounds echoed through the west end of the house, and May rightly surmised that it was Durill at play with the children. When she arrived on the ground she found Parker and old Nurse Joyce shaking with laughter in the doorway of the night nursery. There was big Durill jumping about like a great elephant, and making the room rock again, with fat little Evelyn on his back, and her two short pink legs sprawling over his broad shoulders, while Ivo ran with a whip making the horse go. Both were in their night-clothes, and their pretty curls flying in wild disorder. Nurse Joyce turned to May—

"It is like old times again, Miss May. Lor!

how you two do love these babies. It is a pity but what Mr. Durill had some of his own."

May smiled at the old woman—

" All in good time, Nurse. I dare say you will live to see one of them."

Durill gave one terrific plunge by way of a grand finish, and then dropped into a chair quite out of breath. Evelyn was fast locked in his arms. What a contrast! The strong man, with his short dark curls, just like a little fringe, and the lazy, brown eyes, holding a small creature in a snow-white gown, with light chesnut curls and starry eyes, with her face pressed close against his. Her little hand was patting and fondling him, and twisting in and out of the long beard, while every now and then she would slyly blow in his ear, which event would be followed by a shrill shriek of laughter, and a convulsion of the plump little body, which entirely prevented the night-gown from accomplishing its purpose, after each wriggle it being discovered twisted under her arms. Ivo had had his ride, so May pronounced it time for them to be put into their beds.

" Well, have you enjoyed your ' pig a baggie,' Evelyn?" asked Durill.

" Ris, very much, tank you. You lift Evelyn into bed ?"

" Yes, to be sure ; come along, large party, I can take you too."

Ivo was lifted on the other arm, and in state the two pretty babies were carried to their beds by Durill, May following.

" Now I suppose it is time I betook myself to this gathering, eh May ?"

" Yes, it is, Durill."

May felt very proud of the great big handsome kind-hearted fellow, so ready to amuse and help others, especially little people. She went with him to the court yard, wrapped in a big woollen shawl, to see him off, and watched the last bit of the plain dog cart, with a strap instead of a rail for the back of the seat, disappear. The night was raw and cold, the frost had partly gone, but there was every appearance of snow. The sky had been like lead all day, and now and then one black cloud would set out on a voyage across the heavens. May shuddered, and hailed the cheerful and well-lighted rooms with a feeling of profound satisfaction. Meanwhile Durill was making the best of his way to the village. He got down the hill safely by great care and repeatedly requesting the brown mare to " hold up." Gibbons Grove showed a light or two, but looked particularly dull and chilly, standing back from the road with scarcely any trees in front of it. The weather was not considered sufficiently cold to put the North American bulls under cover, though Durill felt his face getting cut and hacked by the keen snowy wind, and they were congregated round a

not by any means picturesque field pump close
to the hedge, and occasionally giving out a deep
bellow. Near this elegant pump there nearly
always reposed a watering cart, evidently designed
by the same architect—the village wheelwright—
and both these decidedly uncommon construc-
tions were perpetually getting out of order.

Durill dashed up to the Stork, and gave his
horse and trap to an ostler. The bar was to the
right, a snug little place. Durill was well
known there, for he repeatedly called in to have
something hot when he came by the last train—
the quarter to eleven. He strode in, and saluted
the smart barmaid with " How are you, Jenny?
The wind's very biting to-night."

" Yes, indeed it is, Mr. Drever; can I get you
anything, sir?"

" No, thanks; I am bound for this bachelors'
party. Can you tell me where it is going
on?"

"This way, sir; I'll show you," and Miss Jenny tripped away.

I don't believe my knowledge of the Stork will enable me to direct you, notwithstanding the many "Penny Readings" I have attended under its roof. On those occasions we used to mount no end of stairs, and tramp along a passage till we found ourselves in the room. This you must please to remember was the way to the reserved seats. The unreserved were reached by means of a wooden staircase out of the stable yard. But under the able guidance of smart Miss Jenny, Durill found it, and was immediately passed on to a most officious waiter, who bowed and scraped and, amid plenty of "This way if you please, sir," threw open a door and announced him.

Dinner was over, of course, but the gentlemen were warming to their wine, and a peel of mirth met Durill in the doorway. Archer rose and

welcomed him, and the rest exchanged nods.
They were all friends; it was not a particularly
large party, but amongst them there were some
decided specimens. The brothers Hardwick
were there, Mark Calvert, Chandos Stilwell, the
brewer's son; the Rev. James Booth, the lean
curate; Andrew Arckwright, a gentleman staying
in the village to recruit his health after a pro-
tracted sojourn in India; Archer, Crispin, Durill,
and last, but not least, two dear young men,
named respectively Thomas (but better known as
Tommy) Chuckels, and Augustus Gradwell.

Dear Tommy was the only son (at home) of a
doating father and mother. They believed there
never was such a boy as Tommy, and in return
for this belief he gradually developed into a
complete muff. In fact, he was but one remove
from an idiot; only, of course, they had not the
slightest notion of it. He wore coats made by

some antiquated tailor, and slunk about like a young recruit. He followed his mother up and down the house bleating " Ama, ama," like a great sheep.

CHAPTER XIV.

A SMALL boy in a Sunday school was once asked—

"What is the chief end of man?"

To which he replied—

"The end what's got the head on."

That most certainly was not the chief end of Tommy Chuckels; he might as well have had it on the other end for all the use it was to him. It was by no means a bad looking head, though. As far as shape went it promised great things; but, alas! it all ended in promises. He could do nothing but "wear out his shoes," as a lady once said of him. He had a Shakspearian face, a long pointed face, which was, however, robbed of all its beauty by the soft expression that belonged to it. To improve matters he had a sniggering sort of laugh, that many a time, when at the height, was extremely like the bray of a donkey, and just about as musical. Tommy was blessed with a sister, who, thanks be to Providence, possessed a little more sense than himself, and upon the strength of it she sought to protect Tommy, who proved at times extremely unmanageable.

Ellen was dark—a Spanish beauty—of a nervous, irritable temperament; she had long, thin fingers, which, when she was labouring under any strong excitement, twisted and twined themselves together with extraordinary rapidity, and she could wring her hands after a fashion rarely equalled. She was delicate, but according to her own idea she was about to depart at least once a fortnight. The head of this sweet little family was Septimus Chuckels, Esq., a retired merchant, but he did not take upon himself the cares of the household or family. He left that to his wife, a handsome, energetic woman, but penny wise and pound foolish. To make amends for sundry acts of wilful extravagance and slippery deeds, it was Mrs. Chuckels's habit to rake up her family and grand relations, in a soft, lady-like, winning way, that never failed to take. If ever there was fascination in any woman it was Mrs. Chuckels. She was a " shoot " from a good old tree, but she seemed to be under a cloud, as none of that highly respectable family or its numerous branches ever paid her a visit, and Tommy had to waste his marvellous abilities—doing nothing. He was waiting for one of those important personages whom his mother was always writing to, and who had handles to their names, to get him a Government or Staff appointment, to be tacked on to the extremity of some great man's garment, and run after him like a poodle. Tommy could not seek for such employment as is in the reach of

any man, and try with his hands (you perceive I
ignore his head), because his grandfather was
Sir William Walton, and his uncles Sir Somebody
This and Sir Somebody That. So he was waiting
for better times, and thinking he had done a good
day's work when he had shuffled to the post-office
after letters. Indolence predominated in the
Chuckels family, but then they were waiting for
" better times," and running up long bills anywhere and everywhere meanwhile. In all probability dear Tommy is waiting still.

Archer's dinner party made quite a stir at Peak
Hill, because Tommy was asked.

" But I don't think Tommy ought to go, A'ma,"
said wise Ellen.

However, Mrs. Chuckels thought it would be a
capital opportunity of bringing him out, so to the
party at the " Stork " Tommy went in a violent
perspiration.

The other hopeful, Augustus Gradwell, was the

youngest son of a gentleman who had business in London, and to which he went every day, accompanied by his sons. There were some Miss Gradwells, washed-out looking females, and not too young, poor things. Augustus was uncommon, most assuredly. His face was like a girl's, round, and covered with a soft, kittenish down, which he proudly thought of as whiskers and moustache, a downy little dab for a nose, and a mouth pinched up into the form of the letter Q. This young man considered himself nothing short of perfection, and always attired himself in the latest fashion. For one thing he squeezed his spindles of legs into the tightest possible trousers, and his spider body into garments to correspond. Thererefore, sitting perched up driving, or in the back seat behind his father in their double gig, with a flower in his coat, and an eyeglass screwed into one of his pale eyes, nothing ever resembled a dressed-up monkey

more than Augustus Gradwell. He was perpetually falling deeply in love, and would throw
little bunches of flowers, tied with a blue ribbon,
into the garden of the house where dwelt his
angel. The two things desirable to women in
his eyes were an aquiline nose and a long
cervicle vertebræ, which, in comprehensible lan-
guage, means a long neck. He had dipped into
the medical dictionary once or twice, and got off
a few astonishing words, which he ignorantly
thrust into people's faces upon every possible
occasion, and thought that he had impressed them
with a sense of his great learning; it was his
habit to expound at a great length upon subjects
which he knew nothing on earth about, with a
most absurd lisp, which was borrowed of course,
and after a fair quantity of unsuitable words and
bad grammar, wind up with " And that sort of
thing, you know." He earned for himself the
title of " Sweet Fellow," and it was quite a

matter of opinion as to which was the biggest fool, he or Tommy Chuckels.

When Durill arrived on the field, Tommy had already had quite as much wine as was good for him, but he of course had no idea of it, and no one else liked to suggest it. He sat jabbering like a magpie, and relating his wonderful experience and marvellous escapes—from what he did not explain—but it ought to have been, if it was not, from the nearest lunatic asylum.

Augustus Gradwell sat fanning himself with a dinner napkin, a pleased smile on his baby face, and his small eyes turned up.

The rest of the party were jolly enough, but perfectly sensible, and enjoying themselves amazingly. Somebody asked for songs, and Durill was called upon. It was a rare treat to listen to Durill Drever sing; his rich baritone was just splendid, and his ear perfect. He gave them " The Vagabond," in a truly artistic style, and the tender part was rendered faultlessly. George Hardwick followed him with a comic song, which was received with bursts of applause. The time went on, and Tommy had occupied it in drinking everything he could lay his hands on. Mr. Booth started a discussion on theology, but his words were sent back where they came from by Tommy, who scrambled up and informed the company that Booth knew nothing about it, but that he did. And immediately commenced one of the most ridiculously senseless discourses ; hiccupped, slavered, and stammered, and finally fell in a bundle headlong under the table. No one else could get a word in edgeways while he was talking, and at the finish they were all roaring, and George Hardwick pronounced Tommy the best sport out. The clock in the Round House chimed midnight, and directly after the church, and the one in the bar. Then arose the question how was Tommy to be got into the " bosom of his family." Someone must take him, that was quite evident. Captain Hardwick and Durill took hold of him, and commenced shaking him, at the urgent request of Ted Archer, who did not want him to go home in that state.

" I tell you there's nothing like a good shaking; go on, Durill, he'll come to presently."

The shaking he received at the hands of those two strong men was merciless; his teeth chattered, and his addled head rolled so, that short stout Chandos Stilwell, who was as strong as an ox and uncommonly like a prize-fighter, suggested the probability of its coming off. But Archer proved correct; it had the desired effect. His few senses being wound up, and the first use he made of them was to yelp " A'ma ! A'ma !"

Captain Hardwick informed him in the mildest manner possible that he was not his A'ma; but that no doubt his A'ma would be expecting him,

and he had better go home. Chandos Stilwell
and Andrew Arckwright agreed to take him, in
company with the Hardwicks, whose place was
not far from Peak Hill. The rest betook themselves off, laughing and wishing them joy of dear
Tommy. They succeeded in getting him to his
home between them, and then came the momen-
tous question—who was to present him to his
family?

The Hardwicks laughed and begged to be ex-
cused, but promised to hold one of the gates open
and watch over the palings. So Arckwright and
Stilwell had to do it. Now, waiting up for
Tommy were his sister Ellen and a friend—Miss
Bickersteth. They were reading by the fire, or,
at least, Miss Bickersteth was, for Ellen had
fallen asleep on the sofa with her hair all down.
Miss Bickersteth was deep in " Red Court Farm,"
when a fearful falling and fumbling commenced
in the hall; the door was opened, and in came

Tommy staggering. Miss Bickersteth jumped up, exclaiming, " Mr. Chuckels !" in reply to which he made an attempt to throw his arms round her neck, which of course she resisted, and at the same time gave him a push, which, in his helpless condition, sent him sprawling on the floor.

Up got Ellen, wailing—

" Oh, Tommy ! I knew how it would be. I told A'ma. Oh, Tommy !"

At the door appeared fat Chandos, grinning from ear to ear, while smothered bursts of laughter came from the front door, and a voice called out—

" Better carry him up, Chandos."

Chandos needed no second bidding, but took Tommy up as though he had been a baby, and followed by Ellen and Miss Bickersteth, put him on his bed, and said good-night.

In came Mrs. Chuckels in her night-gown, and immediately Ellen pounced upon her with—

"Oh, A'ma, look at Tommy! See, A'ma! I told you so; Tommy ought not to go out. Oh, Tommy!"

The chorus of "Oh, Tommy! Fie, Tommy! For shame, Tommy!" was highly amusing, and Miss Bickersteth enjoyed it.

The upshot of it all was that Tommy was seriously indisposed for the space of two days with what his fond family styled a " bilious attack, dear Tommy not being at all strong."

That dinner party, without doubt, brought Tommy out.

Felton Cottage was once more in a state of commotion. George's regiment was ordered out to India. Captain Hardwick made everything as smooth as possible, and gratified George's every whim. Yet he seemed ill at ease and restless, his great eyes turned incessantly, and fidgetted his calm elder brother dreadfully. But nothing could be drawn from George as to the cause of his trouble. He put no end of obstacles in the way, to prevent his going, and nearly drove his brother distracted.

" George, what are you about? The ' Princess Alice' sails on Saturday, and you are not half ready."

" Never mind, Godwin, it's all right. Let the ' Princess Alice' go without me; I wish to the Lord she would !"

" And then you would be tried by court martial, George, and get into no end of bother. Come, you *must* go, ready or not ready, so you had better set to."

The " set to " was commenced, but it was a poor one; every ten minutes he would take a rest and have a pipe or upset the ink-stand amid his papers. Suddenly forget where he had put a most important thing, and waste half a day looking for it, or seize his French horn, upon

which he could not play a note, and blow such
awful sounds from it as to send the little colony
round the quarry nearly mad.   At last Thursday
arrived, the last day, for he had to meet his regiment at Gravesend on the Friday.   To most of
the people round Maldon he had said adieu, but
when it was close upon five, and quite dusk, he
jumped up, and astonished his brother by telling
him that he was going out for an hour.

" I'll come with you, George."

" No, thank you, Godwin; 1 would rather go
alone.   I sha'n't be long, old fellow."

He turned out, whistling the " Organ Grinder."

It had been raining, and George splashed into
numerous puddles on his way past the quarry.
But he heeded them not, and marched steadily
on down the Dorking Road till he reached Gibbons
Grove.   Then he stopped, and for a second hesi-
tated, but it was soon overcome, for he made a

dash at the gate, and opened it. He reached the front door, and gave a pull at the bell, which was answered by a neat maid.

" Can I see Miss Calvert ?"

" Yes, Mr. Hardwick ; step this way, sir, please."

She evidently understood the difference between Mrs. and Miss, and showed him into the drawing-room without another word.

It was not lighted except by the fire, and that was low, too.

" Miss Calvert! Miss Kate! Ma'am, are you there ? Here's Mr. Hardwick, ma'am."

Kate came forward in the dim uncertain light, and gave her hand to George Hardwick.

" Mamma is not well, Mr. Hardwick, and Ruby is dressing ; but she will not be long, pray sit down."

" Thank you ; don't disturb your sister, Miss Calvert. I—I—came to see you."

"Did you," said Kate, with a nervous little laugh, "how kind of you."

The black eyes looked searchingly at her, and then he said, in a low tone—

"I go away to-morrow, Miss Calvert, and I sha'n't be back for two years; many things may happen in two years, Miss Calvert."

"Yes, many, Mr. Hardwick. I don't suppose you will find things as you leave them on your return."

"No, I suppose not; but I trust I shall find you the same."

Kate laughed.

"No, indeed, you won't, Mr. Hardwick. By-the-bye, do you know Julius Drever comes to Wild Wood in a day or two? He is one of the nicest—"

"Indeed!" answered George Hardwick, stiffly. His voice had a queer rasping sound to Kate, and she turned to him; but he was not looking at her.

They exchanged a few more common-place words, and then he said he must really go, because Godwin would be fidgetty.

"Good-bye, Miss Calvert. I hope that whatever change you make during my absence may be for the better."

He held her hand firmly, then, as if he had suddenly recollected, bowed and turned to the door.

Kate watched his figure disappear down the avenue in the raw, sleety wind, and the tears came into her eyes, and trickled down her rosy cheeks. One slide had dropped in the magic lantern, and shut out the view.

Then Ruby came in with her soft little hands and plump figure, and Kate turned and looked at her with envy in her eyes. Ruby seemed quite contented. Her presence imparted a homely, soft tone to the room, and gave Kate something more to see than a tall, well-knit figure battling its way in the cold, dim night, while the trees sang a mournful lullaby, as if in memory of some-one departed. The North American bulls came to the iron hurdles that fenced off the fields that formed the park, and bellowed miserably. They must have seen the fire light, for Ruby had given it a most energetic poking when she came in, and the ruddy flame went flickering and flashing up the chimney.

" Ruby, will you shut the shutters, dear ?"

Kate did not fancy the bulls staring at her, somehow, to-night.

" Yes, presently, Kate; but I like to see the darkness coming on. What a pity it is we cannot see when evil is coming to us, and shut it out like the night. But May says it is never night, because God gives everyone a light within their own soul."

Kate shivered; she was thinking about her own light that had just been put out.

Ruby went on, with her small paws crossed demurely before her, and enjoying the warmth of the fire—

"I fancy I heard the hall door go to a few minutes before I came down."

"Did you? The wind blew one of the others to, most likely; it seems to be rising to-night."

Kate shivered again.

"Are you cold, Kate? Come and sit here, love. Mamma won't come down, and I am not sorry; she is so cross. So we will have tea together, and fancy it is twenty years hence, when we shall be two angular old maids in earnest."

"Good gracious, Ruby, how you go a-head. If you please I prefer to keep my flesh."

"Then you shall, my dear. Do you know, Kate, I could scarcely help laughing when I went in to see mamma just now. There she is, with an immense poultice of porridge made in a singlet,

spread over her chest, and as far as it will go
almost steamed to death, I should say, from the
look of her face, and giving out the most dismal
moans every now and then, and her eyes turned
up till there's nothing to be seen but the whites.
Butler told me she nearly scalded herself to death
this morning; she turned the huge poultice over,
and the boiling porridge came out. She must be
awfully fond of it, she uses it inwardly and out-
wardly."

Kate smiled.

" Our mother is queer, Ruby."

Ruby gave a grunt, which signified a great deal.

" Kate, play me something, there's a dear girl."

" Not just now, Ruby, I will after tea, which,
by the way, I should imagine to be ready. I
wonder if mamma could not take some ?"

" Bless you no, it would never do for her to
come round too soon, she has not punished
us sufficiently for our cruelty yet."

"No, she will refresh herself with a basin of slops and an inward poultice, and come down to-morrow in a stately manner, followed by a pillow and a hot bottle."

"You will be like her someday, Ruby."

"God forbid," replied Ruby, solemnly. "I do not desire it; I trust He will take me soon, rather than let me become like mamma."

CHAPTER XV.

THEY went into the dining-room and sat down
to a cosy old maid's tea.   Kate managed to partake of some in spite of her sorrow that the
owner of the black eyes had gone, and in a pet
too.   It is only in romances that young women
take to starving themselves when the object of
their tender affections deserts them.   At any rate
the hot cakes and sundry other good things
proved too strong for Kate's feelings.   But then
she was eminently practical, and did not take to
dreaming dreams or seeing visions.   Moreover,
it would rather discourage any young creature,
when indulging in a flight of imagination, to be

asked very suddenly and snappishly, "What are
you thinking about?" Mrs. Calvert was especially fond of doing that; she seemed to consider it part of her maternal duty to be vigilant,
prying, turn her daughters' minds and hearts
inside out if possible, and when they remonstrated,
inform them that "they ought to tell their mother
everything." Nature made a great mistake when
it did not make Mrs. Calvert either a ferret or a
detective.

Kate and Ruby were enjoying their tea famously,
it had been unseasoned with such intelligence as
"Kate! Ruby! ring the bell; run, tell them the
bulls are in the garden!"

"But mamma!"

"Hush, Kate, I can tell by my feelings; and
there won't be a bit of parsley in the morning.
Oh, dear! I don't know what would become of
you without me."

In the midst of the enjoyment of the second

cup the door opened, and in walked Mrs. Calvert, followed by Butler, pillows, shawls, smelling bottles, etc., etc.

Kate and Ruby rose, and wheeled her easy chair to the fire, into which she sank in an exhausted state, and was comfortably settled by the invaluable Butler.

After a few seconds, during which time her nose had been thrust into the fat smelling bottle, Kate ventured to speak.

" We did not expect you down this evening, mamma."

" That is just why I came; I might have been dead for all you cared, ungrateful children ; as it is there is no telling how it will end. Dear me ! there's a dreadful draught from that window."

Neither Kate nor Ruby ventured any difference of opinion to this dismal announcement. The presence of their mother in such an unhappy state of mind acted upon the two girls like a chilling blast, and Kate shivered for the third time that night.

" Kate," said Mrs. Calvert, in a decided tone of voice, " my chest is in a woful state. I am convinced, I feel sure I am coughing my lungs up; I told Butler so."

Ruby's eyes opened to their fullest extent. This was a new feature in her mother's list of ailments, and she had not become used to it. Mrs. Calvert lay back with her eyes closed. She knew she had given them something to digest.

" I think you had better see a doctor to-morrow, mamma ; I will speak to Mark."

" Doctors! No, indeed; I have no faith in doctors, I can do as well for myself. What with homohopathy and hydrophobia—"[" hydro-pathy, mamma," suggested Kate, mildly, while Ruby almost choked, but Mrs. Calvert was riding her hobby and took no notice] " they kill half the people. I only hope and trust I shall let you see what I can do ; if I take after my mother I shall do, who lived to be eighty-three."

Mrs. Calvert need not have distressed herself; she appeared very likely to follow her mother's example. By degrees Mrs. Calvert got better tempered, and Kate rang to have the things removed. The trim maid brought a message from the cook—" Would misses be so kind as to let her go to the village for an hour or two, her mother was going to Dublin, and set off the first train in the morning and wished to see her."

" Yes, Mrs. Calvert would, but she must return by ten."

Ruby bent her steps to the drawing-room and commenced playing. She could not play like Kate but she had some little talent. In a few moments Kate came in with some wool work, and the small fingers stopped, and their owner wheeled round on the stool and faced her.

" There, I did it on purpose; I knew you

would come and stop my miserable strains. Play for me please, Kate; mamma has rubbed me the wrong way."

"Poor pussy cat, what shall I play for it?"

"Anything you choose, only make haste, for there is no telling how long we shall be left in peace, and I will do some of your work for you. How many stitches on this side, Kate?"

"Twenty-four and then twelve chain; mind you keep it even."

Ruby's hands went to work, and the needle went on rapidly. She could work well, indeed it was one of the principal features in the characters of Kate and Ruby that whatever they did they did well, and what they could not do perfectly they left for those who could. Ruby, for instance, always declined to play or sing before people. She would do it to amuse herself or to please Kate, but she would not sit down to perform before a room full of

people. Some persons respected little Ruby Calvert for that it showed great sense; it showed
also that her musical perception was keener than
other people's, because she could detect the least
fault, and she could not think of inflicting hers
upon others. What a pity it is there are not a
few more of Ruby Calvert's way of thinking.
What a deal we should be spared. How often
one's ear is offended and one's nerves set quivering by wrong notes, or a harsh, unfeeling render-
ing of some exquisite melody. You are asked
out to spend the evening and find the room filled,
and of course a piano in one corner. Then
comes the demand for some music, and according
to the rules of society in this highly educated
age, the daughter of the house sets the example,
whether she can or not. Now this fair damsel
has been educated at " The Misses MacSparlin's
seminary for young ladies (the daughters of
gentlemen), Belgravia, Brighton." There they

are supposed to acquire a " superior bearing,"
as the mother of one of these fortunate young
ladies told a girl who was not being educated at
Brighton, and then requested one of her daughters
present to " draw down the blinds lest any one
should be attracted by the valuable pictures on
the walls." No doubt she sought to impress
the young girl by her side, whose position in
life, as regards money, was a step lower, with
a sense of their greatness and her inferiority.
But in that she did not succeed. Two feelings had taken posssession of that girl—contempt and pity. Contempt for the woman
who would be a lady, and whose mind, alas !
was so small, and pity for those pictures—
the offspring of true genius and toil—whose fate
it was to adorn walls where they were neither
understood nor appreciated, except for the actual
money that had been paid for them. So she
rises, without a word of remonstrance, and

spreads herself out before the tortured instrument. There's a terrific crash, and with a splutter and dash she sets off.

For the first page or two you are unable to tell what she is trying to play, but after a bit you get more accustomed to the agonizing sounds, and discover it to be the well-worn " Mazurka des Traineaux ;" but, from some cause or other, she never strikes the correct note through the marked part. She keeps the loud pedal pinned down throughout, and pounds away indefatigably. At last it ends, and the piano goes " Burr, burr ;" but the torture is not over. A young lady is asked to sing—one who has great knowledge of music, and a constant member of the church choir. Wet or fine, she is there, because they could not possibly get along without her. So she stands up in a subdued sort of style (no doubt befitting a member of the choir), and sings " Adaliedia " through her nose. At the close of

this soothing performance her father makes a
circuit of the room, and tells several young ladies,
amid no end of grunts, who are sitting on pins,
that he thinks they had better go with Harriett
to the choir; it is such good practice, and would
improve them so much.

There's a young man standing there who wants
very much to sing, talks about this song and that
song, and in the end, as a matter of course, is
asked if he will sing one.

"Well, really, I don't think I can, but I will
try. I really have got a shocking cold."

By this time he is at the piano, and selects one,
which he tells them is "a beautiful thing—very
difficult." Then he commences with his addled
head thrown back to howl, "Alice, where art
thou?" The young lady who has innocently
volunteered to play his accompaniment cannot
keep up with him. He warms to his work, and
his cracked voice comes in bursts like the wind

through a barn door. After this great effort he is left without any breath for the next bar, and a red face. He cannot even pronounce the Queen's English properly, what with affectation and ignorance, but tells us " The bards (birds) singing gently." What a pity it is someone does not tell that young man he cannot sing ! In all probability he has been told, and been rude to the teller for her or his pains. His self-conceit won't allow him to see for himself. There is nothing like self-conceit for producing blindness and deafness, but it only exists when there is a deficiency of common sense, and what is the use of " knocking when there's no one at home?"

It would be a much better plan for people, when they give those stupid parties and require music, to engage a professional, or only ask those of their guests who *can* play and sing. Music is no music in the hands of some people.

So Kate Calvert commenced to play because

she *could* play, and the blue and white fluffy cap dropped upon Ruby's knee.

Time sped on, and still the cook did not return, so the housemaid went to bed, and Butler had to attend to Mrs. Calvert. Presently she worked herself into a complete fume, and rushed in upon Kate and Ruby.

"What *are* we to do? Cook has never come back, and it is half-past ten, and washing-day to-morrow. Supposing anything has happened to her? Supposing she has been killed?"

"Oh! don't frighten yourself, mamma; she is all right."

"That is *just* like you, Ruby: thoughtless as ever. I wonder what would become of you all if *I* had not had more courage and determination. To think what I have gone through; how I nursed you all when you had measles, and the baby with croup at the same time! Let me see

—yes—that would be you, Kate, and Mark used to hold on by the bed-post. I am quite of a tremble; I might be going on a journey. But you—neither of you—will ever be *half* the woman your mother was!"

"Mamma, don't you think you had better go to bed? Butler, Ruby, and I will stay up and let cook in."

"A likely thing, indeed! I am surprised at you proposing it, Kate!"

And Mrs. Calvert swept out of the room, the picture of injured dignity.

"Dear me!" exclaimed Kate, "why, I thought it was the best thing for her to go to bed."

"So it is, only she is on her stilts to-night; better leave her alone. *I* don't care if cook stays out till two in the morning; it is far nicer here than up-stairs in the cold."

"But the fire will burn out."

" No it won't; I know where to find the coals.
Go on playing, Kate." And Ruby settled herself comfortably.

About eleven there was a ring at the front
door; the back was made up for the night and
no one could get round. In came Mrs. Calvert.

" One of you two go; Butler is putting the
hot bottle in my bed, and it is cook."

Kate went and opened the door, and in stag-
gered the cook, to use a slang term, " as drunk
as a lord."

" My mother's on the stormy ocean (crescendo
of course); my poor old mother."

" Miller, you are not in a fit state to come into
anyone's house," said Mrs. Calvert, keeping as
far from her as possible.

" Ah! yes, bless you, ma'am, quite fit. I have
seen my poor old mother off to Dublin."

" Don't let her have a candle, Kate," whispered Mrs. Calvert, "or we shall all be burnt in our beds."

Kate nodded, and followed her into the kitchen.

"Now, Miller, you are to go to bed; I will put the lamps out."

"You're very kind, Miss, but I must go for some coals."

She reeled round and made a dive at the coal scuttle, the handle of which was, luckily, standing erect. The coals were kept in a cellar, down which there was an immense flight of stone steps, very steep, and not the ghost of a rail. Kate tried to stop her, but it was of no use, go for the coals she would. Ruby had, of course, followed Kate, while Mrs. Calvert stood at the door leading into the servants' offices with clasped hands, ejaculating " Mercy on us!" Now, however, that she saw her begin her perilous descent, she bravely turned back and, catching hold of the handle of the door, commenced repeating the Church service and prayers in a way that would have shamed many a Church clerk. Miller got down safely, wisely performing the journey sitting down mostly, the coal box, of course, going on its own account. After a good deal of scuffling she reappeared, and cleverly crawled up, holding each step with her hands. The coal box contained two small pieces, no doubt it was very well filled when she left the coal heap. Kate and Ruby were thankful when she reached the kitchen. By this time Butler had arrived, and she and Mrs. Calvert relieved themselves of sundry " Disgracefuls," " Abominables," &c. Miller refused to go to bed, and began chanting some Irish song. Mrs. Calvert had a pet dog, a sensible curly little creature, very old; he reposed in a drawer at one side of the dresser on a blanket. It was very like a Pantaloon at times, particularly when frightened, for then his bottom jaw moved up and down incessantly. Toby lay calmly inspecting the scene, and all at once Miller spied " her darling." So she went to him and lifted him out of his bed, saying, " My Mary Ann, in spite of all thy faults I love thee still," and set to work kissing and hugging him violently, much to poor Toby's astonishment and horror. After a great deal of persuasion Miller was got upstairs, having fallen six times by the way, and Mrs. Calvert exclaiming repeatedly, " To think I have lived to see this."

When George Hardwick left Gibbons Grove he dashed through the pools and mud, muttering angrily, " So Miss Chuckels was right after all, and she does like that Julius Drever, —— him ; and before I come back she will be married to him ; bad luck to it all."

" George, wherever have you been to? You

are splashed all over. Surely the village street is not so bad as all that."

" I don't know, I am sure, Godwin; I never noticed it, to tell the truth."

" Then where did you go to ?"

" The Post Office," answered Mr. George, composedly, without blinking an eyelid.

He was very surly, sat smoking and drinking far into the night, and then left the little village by the early train—half-past six. His brother saw him off, and then returned to the quiet of his little cottage, quite satisfied that he had not neglected George in any possible way, and thinking he was rather a strange fellow after all. And the train flew on to London, carrying in one of its first-class compartments a tall, dark man, with black, straight hair combed flat against each side of his head, and looking not unlike some noted violin player, but for the unmistakeable military cut about him. He sat very still, sometimes nibbling his moustache and looking at his watch. Then he thought of his passage to India—the life he would lead out there—and what when he came back. He had once said to Kate Calvert—

" If I don't marry and settle down when I come home, I shall go to the dogs."

His ideas would not carry him past the time when he should come home—he saw Kate Mrs. Julius, and his tanned face turned a yellowish white—he seemed to meditate springing away from his misery, and opened the window to get some air, the carriage felt so close. Then he saw he was at London Bridge, and the people stirring about, and when the door was unlocked with a click, he got out and stood on the platform in the chilly morning air.

END OF VOL. I.

T. C. NEWBY, 30, Welbeck Street, Cavendish Square, London.